P9-BIJ-955

BILLY BAYES

BILLY BAYES

•

TOM CLARKE

CLARKE
c.1

AVALON BOOKS
THOMAS BOUREGY AND COMPANY, INC.
401 LAFAYETTE STREET
NEW YORK, NEW YORK 10003

PRINTED IN THE UNITED STATES OF AMERICA
ON ACID-FREE PAPER
BY HADDON CRAFTSMEN, SCRANTON, PENNSYLVANIA

To Thomas Joseph

Chapter 1

Billy Bayes came riding in from the snow-covered foot-hills of the Sangre de Cristos one clear afternoon during the first seasonal thaw, and under ordinary conditions Josh Clemens, the ramrod at the Rocking J, would have thrown a fit and sent the kid packing back to his isolated line shack until the annual spring roundup. But it had been no ordinary winter in those parts, neither in the high country nor out on the open range, and old Clemens, despite his feigned toughness when dealing with the youngest of his hands, could sympathize with him for the unusual hardships he must have endured for those few months in the frigid high country.

According to most of the old-timers at the Rocking J, there had never been, in their collective memories, a winter to quite match the severity of this last one, and among the dozen or so hands who gathered around the bunkhouse stove each night to chew the fat, all but a couple expressed their doubts that the kid would survive the entire winter in that old line shack.

And it was rumored by those same doubters that after enough snow had melted in the high country to make the line shack accessible to horses, straws would be drawn among them to see who would have the unsavory task of riding up there and removing the kid's frozen remains to the ranch for a proper burial.

So it was with a certain personal relief that old Clemens

watched from the window of his private quarters near the bunkhouse as Billy Bayes rounded the corner of the south corral and headed straightaway for the barn.

As the weary kid dismounted and swung open the barn door, leading his horse inside, Clemens could tell by his body language alone that he was in a mood, and the wise old ramrod was knowledgeable enough of the ways of cowboys to recognize when to check his temper when dealing with them—and this was surely one of those times, he surmised at a glance. Besides, the old man had worried so about the safety and comfort of the kid these last weeks of winter that he was plumb tickled just to see him ride in with his extremities still intact.

With his hands in his pockets and an unaccustomed casualness, Clemens left the warmth of his shack and ambled out to the barn where he found Billy wiping down his chestnut gelding with handfuls of dry hay.

Grinning broadly, the ramrod handed Billy some fresh hay and said, "Right nice day, ain't it?"

"Better than some, I reckon."

"Uh . . . where's your pack animal, kid?"

"Snowed in without supplies . . . had to eat him."

"Said what?"

"Et him."

"Oh . . . well. That bad up there, was it?"

"Yep."

"Count many strays in the hills?"

"Not the first one."

"Why's that?"

"Blizzard got them."

"Every dang one of 'em?"

"Every dang one of 'em."

"Must have been even worse up there than I figured, huh?"

"I reckon."

"Want to talk about it right now?"

"Maybe later."

"Well ... been nice palavering with you, kid. When you're finished, come inside where it's warm, and Cookie'll rustle you up a big steak and some hot biscuits."

"Thanks."

"Don't mention it."

Now to a casual observer who didn't know the two men well, one old enough to be the other's pa, the conversation between them in the barn might seem an ordinary exchange of pleasantries and information between a working ramrod and one of his young hands, but little would that same observer have guessed, merely by the politeness of the exchange, that the two amiable-appearing cowboys were perhaps the most hot-tempered men in the entire territory of New Mexico, and that it was only through a concerted effort on both their parts that the exchange managed to come off without a commotion.

That old Josh Clemens had a paternal fondness for the young Billy was an indisputable fact among the close-knit Rocking J hands, and they were equally cognizant of the fact that the tough old ramrod played no favorite with the kid, insofar as his duties around the ranch were concerned, leastways.

It was quite the opposite, actually, in that Clemens pushed the young cowboy to the very limits of his abilities and endurance, loading him with enough chores to keep him busy from sunup until sundown, never seeming to cut him enough slack time to figure out that he was actually carrying the workload of two average hands.

But it would belie the fact to say that Billy wasn't smart enough to figure out on his own that he was doing much more than his fair share of the work around the Rocking J. What did seem to slip past his understanding, however, was that the ramrod had long ago recognized in Billy the potential of becoming one of the best all-around cowboys ever, and that he was being pushed to perform under the most extreme conditions in order to hone his skills for that inevitable day when he might find himself in an unusually tough situation, and the old man would not be there to do his thinking for him.

To say that Billy accepted without question every task given him by the ramrod was altogether another story. Such snorting and bellowing you never heard when the kid and the old man went toe-to-toe over a repetitious chore that the kid thought should have been given one of the other hands instead of himself.

When Billy was sent to mend fences days on end, for instance, he could likely be expected to stand up to Clemens and complain in no uncertain terms that he had done little else but repair fences for the last two weeks or so, and it was dang well high time he drew a chance to ride herd, or search for strays, or run into town for supplies—just about any old thing to get off fence work for a while.

And old Clemens, his hands on his hips and his sun-bronzed jaws working a generous chaw, would hunch forward with his face inches from Billy's and let roar that he was going to work fences until he learned to do the thing like it ought to be done, and, what's more; if he didn't like it, they were hiring next door at the Dobie Girl spread.

Yet, in spite of all his foot-stomping and bellyaching, Billy would grin boyishly and tip his hat at the red-faced ramrod and mount his chestnut for yet another day on the fences. He would approach his assigned chore with such a sense of purpose, enthusiasm, and dedication that those who had been assigned to work with him were generally left bewildered by the shift in his attitude.

And after Billy would mount his horse and ride off to perform his day's chores, the grinning old ramrod would slap his leg with his hat and shake his head in mock exasperation and say, to no one in particular, "That kid is going to make one hell of a cowboy some day."

Clemens took Billy's blow-ups and bullheadedness in stride, and wrote off the frequent confrontations as his way of seeking attention. And knowing that the kid looked on him as a father figure of sorts and expected a periodic dressing down from time to time, he never failed to accommodate him, and most usually gave him a chewing that any errant son might expect from a concerned father.

Possessed of strong paternal instincts, but not having sons of his own, Josh took particular interest in green youngsters like Billy, taking the time and patience to teach them the ways of successful ranching. And no natural father was any prouder of his "boys" when they finally reached that stage in their training when the old ramrod considered them the caliber of men who could now perform under the harsh conditions of the New Mexico rangeland without his direct supervision.

And of all his countless proteges over the years, Josh was most proud of Billy Bayes, who, in his opinion, held promise of becoming the most well-rounded cowboy he had ever had the pleasure of working with.

Now old Josh didn't come to be the ramrod of one of the largest and most successful ranching operations along the Canadian because of his chronological years, or by chance— far from it. He was in his position because he knew the

workings of a ranch like few in those parts ever had, and
he also had a keen instinct for judging the worth and ca-
pabilities of the men on his payroll.

So it was with the greatest of confidence, when Paul
Sanderson, the owner of the Rocking J, asked who was the
best all-around hand on the place, that Josh replied, "Why,
that would be Billy Bayes, Paul, without a doubt in my
mind."

"Young Billy, you say. Yes, I have observed his performance over the years, Josh, and I quite agree that he is
an extraordinary wrangler and cowhand, and considering
the fact that he was wilder than a green-broke colt when he
first arrived here, I'd have to commend you for the outstanding hand he has become. But gosh darn it, Josh, he's
so . . . young."

"He's sure that, Paul, but in all the years we've known
each other, have I yet steered you wrong about a man?
Agreed he ain't more'n a kid, but I'd trust that Billy can
out-best any older hand on the place, and that's saying a
mouthful, because we both know that the Rocking J has as
fine a crew as any spread in these parts."

"I'll give you that, Josh. You know your men all right,
and I'll be the very first to admit that I owe the success of
the Rocking J in part to the crew on my payroll. But the
job I have in mind is one of a personal nature, and is one
I would ordinarily handle myself."

Pointing at his stocking feet resting on a padded ottoman,
he said, "This damn gout of mine picked a fine time to act
up on me, just when I had something of the greatest importance to take care of in Bent Rock. I daresay the man
you recommend for this job will be acting in my stead."

"I got no idea what this job is you're leading up to, Paul,

but I'll stake my reputation that young Billy can handle it as well as any older hand on the place—if not better.''

"That's good enough for me, Josh. You send him in to see me this evening, and I'll go over the details with him personally.

"And as long as you're here, I'll take this opportunity to fill you in on my future plans for the Rocking J. As we both know, Josh, the Rocking J runs one of the finest strings of broodmares in the territory, but I've been thinking there's still room for improvement in the herd. Now I haven't the vaguest idea how all this is going to work out, but I've purchased an Arabian stallion to use experimentally here at the ranch. Horse breeding is becoming competitive in these parts lately, as you're well aware, and to stay on top of it a man has to remain open to new ideas.''

"Whew! An Arabian, you say. I heard about them, but I never saw one myself. Expensive, too—so I've been told.''

"Extremely expensive, Josh, if you want the truth of the matter. Now you can begin to see why I want our best wrangler for this job. With my hopes for the future of the Rocking J depending on this stallion, I daresay I won't feel comfortable until he's safely stalled here at the ranch.

"You never did meet my daughter Rebecca before she went to live with my sister in Baltimore. That was the year before you hired on here. But you probably recall my telling you about her ma passing away when Becky was no more than nine years old, and at the time I didn't think the ranch to be a proper environment for a little girl—you know, not having the influence of a woman and all. So my sister Effie insisted on taking her in while she pursued her education.

"Becky is finished with her schooling now, and she and my sister will be accompanying the Arabian to Bent Rock.

My sister plans to spend the summer here at the ranch before returning to Baltimore.

"So you see, Josh, your man will be responsible for meeting my family and the Arabian at the train depot in Bent Rock and seeing them safely to the ranch. Bent Rock, as you well know, is a good two-day ride by wagon, and although I hardly anticipate any problems along the way, you can begin to see why I insist on having your best wrangler to act in my stead."

"I ain't changed my mind in the least, Paul. I realize you're talking a powerful responsibility, what with your ladies involved—and that expensive horse—but I'll stick to my original recommendation that Billy Bayes is the man for the job."

"Splendid, Josh, we'll go with that. Now, while you're here, we need to discuss that recurring problem of missing cattle. I realize the loss is insignificant for a spread of this size, but considering what the blizzards did to the herd up in the hills, we need to find a way to cut our losses at the hands of that half-breed, Lupe."

"I've studied the problem, Paul, and it's like I told you before, he's only taking those few cattle that happens to stray off your range, and the way I see it, if we tighten up on the herd to the south of us we can put him out of business altogether. The wily varmint is much too shrewd to show himself on the open range."

"Even giving him a few head is more than I wish to lose right now. After the significant losses out here to the recent cold weather, I expect to see an increase in beef prices, and every head we keep out of his thieving hands is money in the bank. Do whatever you have to do to keep the herd bunched up on the south range."

"I'll take a couple of hands off the west range. Anything

that crosses over to the Dobie Girl spread will be returned to us come spring roundup.''

"That sounds good to me, Josh. Whatever it takes to cut our losses to those pesky rustlers.''

When old Clemens had anything serious to ponder, he most usually rode out a short distance to the south corral and cut himself a chew of Burley, propping his feet on the watering trough and gazing out on the open range. There, in all that vast quietness, with only the creaking noises of the windmill to break the stillness, he most generally found himself able to reason out a palpable solution to whatever problem brought him there.

Seems there was something about the wide expanse of open range and the distant peaks of the Sangre de Cristos, and even the creaking noises of the derelict windmill, that never failed to lift his spirits and enhance his thinking process.

And so big a part did the creaky old windmill play in his ritual that he was once fit to be tied when a new hand took it on himself to apply grease to the rusting mechanism, causing Josh's thoughts to go helter skelter. After that greasing, Josh had a sign posted on the windmill that it was never to be greased again—much to the puzzlement of the newer hands.

On this particular evening Josh ruminated over his earlier conversation with the ranch owner. He had all the confidence in the world in his youngest hand, both as a man and a wrangler, but overseeing the safe delivery of the Sanderson ladies and a horse that had to be worth more than all the horses on the place lumped together left him with an unsettled feeling in the pit of his stomach.

He hoped he wasn't putting his job on the line by rec-

ommending the kid. After all, the kid had little experience
with anything but ranching, as far as he knew, and this was
a job that required the delicate handling of fine ladies, ladies
of the type that Billy had not been exposed to while working
for the Rocking J.

"You worry too much, Josh," he said over the noise of
the creaky windmill. "It's a done thing." He had made a
gut decision and by cracky he would stand behind it—
whatever the outcome.

Approaching Billy in the bunkhouse, Josh couldn't help
noticing the kid's sunken cheeks and sallow complexion,
the result of his ordeal in the mountains. Though the kid
made no outward complaint about his isolation in the remote
line shack, Josh could tell it had been rougher up there than
anyone could imagine. Suddenly he felt well justified in his
decision to recommend Billy for the trip to Bent Rock. If
any one hand on the place deserved a vacation from ranching
duties it was the kid. And if the first man made a remark
about his playing favorites with the young hand, that man
would answer to his wrath.

"Say, kid, now that you're back and rested up, there's
something you'll have to take care of for the boss." Josh
tilted his hat and grinned down at Billy.

Studying Josh's words for a moment, Billy jumped
quickly to his feet and squared off with the ramrod with an
expression that Josh knew only too well. "Now just you
look, boss, you know I've been up in those hills since early
January, and I had to cut a hole in the roof of that drafty
line shack when it snowed under. On top of that, I had to
barbeque my favorite pack horse just to have food enough
to survive until the snow thawed. And you haven't even
heard the worst of it—"

"Whoa there, kid. Just you hold on and don't start getting

yourself in a dither. I'm not here to lay another chore on you so soon after what you been through up there. No, sir, we need to discuss something entirely different.''

"Oh, no,'' Billy said, turning a slow circle and shaking his head. ''Sanderson found out about that fracas I had in the Golden Girl Saloon last November, didn't he? I've been paying for all that damage, boss. Look, I even have receipts to prove it—''

"Ain't that either. But remind me sometime to inquire about that fracas. Ought to be real interesting hearing your side of it. No, what I'm really here to talk about is your vacation. I think you need a couple of weeks off after all those months in the hills.''

"A vacation? Did somebody slip some loco weed in your chewing tobacco, boss? Cowboys don't take vacations. You're setting me up for something, aren't you? And what does Sanderson have to do with it?''

"No, it's true, kid. Sanderson wants you to take a couple of weeks in Bent Rock before escorting his ladies to the Rocking J. If you can't handle it, I'll find at least a dozen hands around this place who'd plug their best friend to make that trip.''

"Me? Sanderson wants me to escort his ladies from Bent Rock? Why, I didn't know he had any ladies. Everybody knows his wife died of consumption some years back. Now wait a doggone minute, boss . . . does this mean I have to procure ladies for Mr. Sanderson—all the way from Bent Rock? The ladies at the Golden Girl aren't good enough for him?''

"I'll finish what I started to say before you mounted your fantasy horse, kid. The ladies I'm talking about are Sanderson's daughter and sister, out of Baltimore. You best get used to the idea of having ladies around the place from now on.''

"Yeah, come to think of it, I do remember hearing rumors about Sanderson having a little girl somewhere back East.''

"Well, she's not so little now. If I had to take a wild guess, I'd say she would be your age about now, or a mite younger. And if you get any ideas—''

"Ideas? With Sanderson's daughter? Hold your tongue, boss. She's probably some spoiled, over-educated little brat with back-East ways, and I seriously doubt I'd be interested—even if she turned out to be otherwise.''

"Glad to hear it, kid. Now go talk to the boss after a while. He wants to fill you in on your trip to Bent Rock. And kid, clean yourself up a mite before you go to the main house—and shave those whiskers off. And don't forget to knock first . . . and remove your hat indoors. . . . ''

"I don't need instructions about manners, boss. Give me some credit, will you. After all, I do make it into town now and then.''

"Oh, sure, you make it into town, kid—the Golden Girl Saloon. The sort of manners you're apt to pick up at that place don't hardly count in polite company. I'm afraid I've been so all-fired busy making you into a cowboy, that I've been neglect of teaching you the manners you'll need around fine folks.''

"Just when is this trip into Bent Rock suppose to come off, boss? Did Mr. Sanderson say?''

"Clean yourself up and go talk to him, kid. He'll say.''

Clutching his hat tightly in his hand, a very nervous, slicked-up Billy knocked on the kitchen door of the main house and waited. Seldom did the hands enter the living quarters of the ranch owner, and he had been inside the house only once in all the four years he had worked for

Sanderson. A couple of years back, he had been sent to help uncrate fine pieces of mahogany furniture from back East. Not accustomed to such luxury as he saw in the house, he couldn't relax all the time he was there, fearing he would brush against some expensive piece of artwork and send it crashing to the floor. He'd be relieved when finally the chore was completed and he was back in the familiar surroundings of the bunkhouse.

Chang Lo, Sanderson's personal cook and houseboy, opened the door and beamed up at Billy. "Ah, Mr. Billy. Mr. Sanderson wait for you in library. Please, you follow Chang Lo."

The old Chinaman, a leftover from the early railroad-building days, was dressed in Western clothes, although he still retained his impressive queue, which was decorated with a red bow and swung from side to side as he led Billy hurriedly down the high-ceilinged hallway.

Billy was ushered into a book-filled room as large as the bunkhouse and formally announced to Paul Sanderson. He had never seen so many books in his entire life, and felt it must something akin to sacrilege for only one man to own so many volumes for his own reading pleasure. What he himself wouldn't give to have access to the books from time to time.

Paul Sanderson, in his late fifties, large of build, bearded and balding, was sitting in an over-stuffed chair with his feet resting on an ottoman, and in his lap was a book which he closed when Billy was announced.

"Billy," the older man said warmly, "it has been a long while. Do sit down, please." He indicated a chair directly across from him. "I'm about to have coffee, will you join me?"

"No, thank you, sir. I'm fine."

"Billy Bayes," the man said almost to himself, focusing his attention on the kid and studying him like a curiosity. "I vaguely remember when Josh first brought you to the Rocking J. About four years ago, wasn't it?"

"About that, I reckon."

"You were just a skinny little kid then, as I recall, but I can see where that no longer holds true. You've grown into quite the man these days. How tall would you say you are now, about six feet?"

"Yes, sir, something like that." Billy wished the man would get on another subject; such attention to himself only made him self-conscious and uncomfortable.

"Josh Clemens holds you in rather high regard, you know. From the build-up he gave you earlier I half expected you to be about seven feet tall by now." He chuckled at his own wit, and Billy could feel a flush come to his cheeks. Acknowledging the remark inarticulately, Billy laughed along with the ranch owner.

"Now, Billy, let's get down to the reason why you're here." He took a sip of coffee and made a wry face, looking up at Billy with a serious, businesslike expression showing through his whiskers. "Josh tells me that you're the best wrangler on the place—you're blushing, Billy, but it's true he feels that. He happens to be the best judge of men I've ever had the honor of knowing. If he says you're the one for the job, I'll accept that recommendation without question.

"My daughter Rebecca—we call her Becky—and my sister Effie are due to arrive by train in about three days. You will take the buckboard to Bent Rock and be there waiting for them when their train arrives.

"Also, there is the matter of a horse. Not an ordinary horse, I might add, but a very expensive stallion from Arabia which will arrive on the same train as the ladies. I cannot overstate the importance of this horse to the future plans of the Rocking J, and I shall expect you to give this horse very special care and attention while en route to the ranch. Do you think you can handle the responsibilities as I've explained them?''

"I see no problems there, sir."

"Fine. I don't think you will have any problems. Oh, there are yet a few renegades around, as well as a few outlaws, but for the most part they have been confined to the high country, and they're mostly into rustling a steer or two—nothing that either of us should be concerned about, I should think.

"But just to be on the safe side, I shall want you to be alert at all times, both in Bent Rock and on the open trail. If there is one thing we can be certain of in this country, it is that we cannot be certain of anything. Do you understand all this so far?"

"Yes, sir, I understand perfectly."

"Very well. This is something I would normally take care of myself, but my gout picked a fine time indeed in which to act up on me," the ranch owner said, waving a hand at his feet.

"Because the long trip across the country by train can be terribly tiring, as you can imagine, the ladies will spend an extra week or so in Bent Rock. This is partly to allow them to rest up from their arduous trip, and partly to allow the Arabian the time to acclimate to his new surroundings before making the journey to the ranch. This has all been prearranged with my daughter and sister.

"As to your expenses," he said, tossing Billy a heavy leather pouch, "that should be enough gold to cover any unforeseen emergency. I have no problem with your staying at the best hotel or eating in the finest restaurants, but I do expect an accounting of your expenses when you return. Do you have any questions?''

"Just one, sir. How will I recognize your daughter and sister?''

"Oh, you will recognize them, to be certain. My daughter has taken it upon herself the responsibility for the care of the Arabian while in transit. If you should happen to miss them at the train depot, they will be staying at the Tivoli Hotel.''

Chapter 2

An excited Billy Bayes finished tying his chestnut to the buckboard and climbed aboard to beam down at Josh Clemens. That Josh had had a sleepless night was apparent by his slouched shoulders and the heavy puffiness around his eyes, and he paced nervously about as the kid studied every detail of the fancy wagon like it was a new toy.

"Now, Billy, you sure you got all of Mr. Sanderson's instructions in your head? You ain't forgetting nothing, are you?"

"You know, Josh, you're one more fine ramrod. The very best, and a better friend this young cowboy never had. But dang it all, you worry too much. As one friend to another, I really think you need to make it into town more often. I'm becoming concerned about you."

"And you think a trip into town is the answer, kid?"

"I do, boss. I think you should give serious consideration to visiting the Golden Girl Saloon and checking out what goes on in those upstairs rooms. I'm truly concerned for your health."

The old ramrod slowly removed a plug of chewing tobacco from his pocket, cut himself a generous chaw, and looked up at Billy as he said, "Kid, if you don't have that rig out of here by the time I take a good spatshot, it'll be the state of *your* health that's under discussion."

"In that case, I'm out of here, boss. See you in a couple of weeks. Hyup there, hoss!"

On the open trail, Billy was flying free. He couldn't remember when he had felt so exhilarated and unfettered. Before him lay the road to Bent Rock. Tonight he would bed down in a one-hotel town called Las Cumbres, his midway point. Tomorrow afternoon, barring any unforeseen problems to slow him down, he would have himself a soft bed in the fanciest hotel in Bent Rock.

And judging from the weight of the pouch of double eagles that Sanderson had given him, he would be going first class all the way. One thing could be said of the wealthy, he mused, they were so accustomed to luxury that they had developed the mistaken notion that everybody lived as they did—which most likely accounted for the excess of gold given him. Well, he would not disappoint his boss. He would find some way to spend a good part of the money.

Never had Billy traveled this particular part of the country. When he did chance to leave the confines of the Rocking J, it was to seek entertainment in the Golden Girl Saloon in Sayers Flat, a small community just north of the ranch that existed primarily to supply the needs of the many surrounding ranches. The country he now traveled being new to him, he relished the sights like any newcomer who was seeing northeast New Mexico for the first time.

In the four years or so that he had worked on the Rocking J, Billy had never taken off from his job for more than a couple of days at any one time, and felt that he deserved the trip to Bent Rock as much as any hand on the place.

He thought back to that night, four years ago, when he had found himself stranded in this country without food and money, and how Josh Clemens chanced upon his camp at night, and how that meeting ultimately led to his job with the Rocking J.

He had come a long way since that meeting with the kindly old ramrod, and he really couldn't say whether to attribute it to circumstance or fate, but Billy knew that he could never go back to the life he had led before coming to the Rocking J.

Being the only child of a consumptive east-Kansas dirt farmer, Billy's early years were those of perpetual hunger and deprivation. His pa, on his good days, would work whatever he could of their hardscrabble farm, but his good days were exceedingly rare, and his ma could only do so much to keep the crops in the ground. Between his parents, it seemed to Billy, they had often fallen short of providing a decent living for themselves and their only child.

It was when Billy was seven years old that his pa finally succumbed to the illness which had sapped his strength over the years. He could still remember helping his distraught ma bury him unceremoniously in a shallow grave behind the barn, wrapped in a blanket, and marked with a cross fashioned from old boards.

For three years after the death of his pa, Billy and his ma struggled to hold the mortgaged farm together, but bit by bit it was borrowed against without the means of repaying the loans, until, finally, the entire property—land, livestock, and personal belongings—was repossessed by the local bank, and they were left with no choice but to move in with his ma's older brother, an alcoholic with an obese wife and six young daughters to feed.

Life was no better for them at his uncle's place. Being the only male in the household, besides his soused uncle, Billy was soon forced to do a man's job in the fields, walking behind a team of scrawny mules from first light to first dark, trying to coax from an effete soil a living for a hungry family of ten.

Never experiencing the fun and games of other children his age, Billy soon found his existence to be no more exciting than that of the mules that he followed day on end. And then he discovered reading.

At night, by the light of a candle, his ma taught him to read from the family bible, helping him to pronounce the strange, tongue-twisting names and places that held no meaning to a lad whose only world was a square of land that threatened to shackle him to the same unyielding yoke as that of his pa before him.

But he persisted, with his ma's encouragement, to study the bible, until at last he could make his way through the scriptures without her assistance.

When he was twelve years old, Billy chanced upon a barrel of leather-bound books which had been mysteriously abandoned beside a wagon trail in the middle of the prairie. And from the moment when he opened the first book and began to read, he dreamed of a world with limitless horizons.

Billy's final tie to his uncles's hated farm was severed when his ma died unexpectedly of pneumonia. When the eulogy was read and the final scoop of dirt was thrown on her resting place, he began to make plans to head west in search of a better life for himself.

His opportunity to leave the farm and seek adventure came unexpectedly several days later, when a supply train made up of mule teams camped near the farm for the night. Inquiring of the wagon boss, Billy was informed that the train was heading for Santa Fe, following the original trail, which had all but been abandoned since the advent of the railroad.

As tall at fifteen as a full-grown man, Billy was immediately hired to accompany the wagon train to its destination, doing a man's job for a man's pay. The job of mule whacker, for which he was hired, paid twenty dollars a month and meals, undreamed of money for a fifteen-year-old Kansas dirt farmer. Because of a lifetime of experience with stubborn mules, it was a job he fit into naturally, and from the moment when he swung his possible bag into the wagon and released the brakes and took up the whip, he began to experience some of life rather than reading about it.

The mule whackers with whom Billy traveled were a coarse lot, and around the campfires at night and in the small towns where they sought solace in the arms of equally coarse women, he was introduced to a side of life that went against every principle earlier instilled in him by his Christian parents.

On the trail, Billy learned to defend himself with his fists, to size up a man on first encounter, and to see through the feigned affections offered him by the many painted ladies whom he met in the endless number of saloons and bawdy houses along their route.

By the time the wagon train reached Santa Fe, Billy had become totally disillusioned with the life of a mule driver, a life which in the beginning had appeared to be his ticket to the many adventures he had so often dreamed of as a youth. He realized along the route that what he really longed for was a place where he belonged, a place where he could finally put down roots and become a part of the viable family he had never really had.

Taking what remained of his pay, Billy purchased a swayback piebald mare and a .44 six-gun and headed for Albuquerque, looking over the vast country and asking for work at the many ranches in the surrounding area.

But times were not good for the ranchers, and they declined to hire a green kid who had never worked cattle. From there he headed east, crossing the Pecos just south of the Sangre de Cristos, then northeast toward the Canadian.

Along the Canadian Billy was reduced to eating jackrabbits without salt after his money and supplies had been used up. Sometimes he knocked on doors, still seeking work, and was only given small chores in exchange for meals.

Sitting close to his campfire late one night because of the cold of the approaching winter, hungry, and thinking that even a jackrabbit would have tasted good about them, he was hailed from the darkness by an old cowboy, who asked if he might warm his hands.

The man was well provided and he shared his rations with the starving kid. They conversed like old friends, talking well into the late hours of the night, and by the time they spread their blankets they had found each other acceptable.

The next morning Billy was taken to the Rocking J and introduced to Paul Sanderson, who put him on the payroll, solely on the recommendation of Josh Clemens, who convinced the ranch owner that he could see much promise in the green kid.

Four years had elapsed since that night by the fire, and Billy had oftentimes felt that providence had intervened to secure for him a place at the Rocking J, and in the overall scheme of things he was exactly where he was meant to be.

Chapter 3

Billy took his nooning in a small copse near a running stream that ran parallel to the trail. The cold lunch the cook had placed in the buckboard was enough to feed several men over, and he virtually stuffed himself to excess, remembering, perhaps, that period in the line shack when he was so long without provisions and had to survive on horse-flesh. He napped against a cottonwood tree and allowed the horses to graze on the lush grass that grew along the creek.

Waking refreshed, he watered the horses once more and resumed his trip toward Las Cumbres. Judging by the position of the sun, he was making good time, and he expected to be at his halfway point on schedule.

By the time he entered Las Cumbres and drew up in front of the livery, Billy's early enthusiasm for the trip had begun to wane. The buckboard, he finally determined along the way, was not a means of conveyance meant for extended trips over the rough terrain and rock-strewn trail he had traveled. To a cowboy accustomed to sitting the saddle, the jolting wagon was taking its toll on both his body and his patience.

Seeing first to the care of the horses, Billy enlisted the help of the livery man in removing the wheels from the buckboard and applying a new coat of grease to the axles. His chores out of the way, he rented accommodations at

the town's only hotel and removed the trail dust from himself
in preparation for his evening meal.

Picking at the rich food set before him in the hotel's
adjoining dining room by a bored and surly waiter, Billy at
once realized he wasn't that hungry after all. It was only
because Sanderson was paying his expenses that he had
decided to experiment with the likes of roast quail and
buffalo tongue. The rough ride in the buckboard had tired
him out and left him without much of an appetite.

Leaving his meal only partially eaten, Billy trudged up
the stairs to his room and retired early. All his previous
plans in regards to whooping it up once he reached Las
Cumbres were cast aside in favor of obtaining a good night's
rest in order to recover from his exhausting trip. Maybe in
Bent Rock, he thought, losing himself to sleep.

In the dining room the next morning, three unkempt men
who appeared to be traveling companions shared the long
table with Billy. Having become adept at judging strangers
on sight, he felt uneasy in their presence. Upon being seated
by the waiter, he only nodded curtly to the men and studied
the menu in silence.

The men, a hard-looking lot, studied Billy for a moment,
and finding him of no interest, ignored his presence while
they conversed among themselves in monosyllabic whis-
pers.

The three men were filthy with road dirt, and their wide-
rimmed range hats were weathered and torn and coated with
a fine white dust. The odor of stale perspiration hung in the
air and seemed to permeate the entire dining room.

Billy could not enjoy his food because of the smell, but
he managed to control the nausea he felt while he wolfed
down his breakfast in his haste to get it over with and seek
the fresh air of the outdoors. However, he did not wish to

openly offend the strangers by appearing to be in too big a rush to remove himself from their presence; he had heard of men dying at the hands of strangers for even lesser slights.

Breathing the free air at last, Billy left Las Cumbres in the saddle, leading the bay pulling the buckboard. Now, on horseback, his earlier enthusiasm for the trip returned, and he was looking forward to spending the night in the fanciest hotel in Bent Rock. His spirits soared as he cut through the juniper- and piñon-covered foothills toward his final destination.

Finally, after an uneventful day of riding, Billy entered the outskirts of Bent Rock in the late afternoon. On the very periphery of the town he was met by the sight of the ever-present adobe huts of the poor, leading him to believe that Bent Rock would be just another necessary commercial blight on the landscape, but as he progressed along the main street leading into the heart of town, the homes began to take on the appearance of affluence, some even rivaling those homes of the larger cities in their splendor and opulence.

Billy found himself riding through a veritable modern town, with dozens of fine stores and hotels and saloons of every description bordering the main street. Prominently situated in the town square was a brand-new opera house, with banners announcing the upcoming appearance of Miss Jenny Lind.

Finding a livery stable near the Tivoli, Billy made arrangements for the horses and buckboard, then swung his warbag over his shoulder and made his way along the crowded sidewalk to the hotel, where he would be staying while in town.

At the Tivoli he registered for a week and was shown to a luxurious room which surpassed all his preconceived notions of what a big-city hotel room should be. In the direct center of the big room was a large canopied bed which could possibly accommodate a family of six, and on either side of the carpeted room were various overstuffed chairs and tables that bespoke wealth.

Suddenly he was overawed by the fine furnishings and wished he had settled for a less expensive hotel. But it was only a passing thought, for he remembered the ranch owner himself had recommended the hotel, and had provided the gold with which to pay for it.

Tipping the man who showed him the room, Billy ordered a bath and threw his warbag on the big bed. If Mr. Sanderson had intended for him to go first class, he would certainly do everything in his power not to disappoint the man.

Relieved now of the road dirt, Billy suddenly felt conscious of his faded jeans and shirt, and set out at once to correct the deficiency in his wardrobe. Using his own money that had accumulated while he languished all winter in the line shack, he purchased new clothes, and a wide-rimmed range hat that was all the rage.

Now, shaved, shined, and wearing a new outfit that had cost him three month's wages, Billy purchased a fair-to-middling cigar and joined the strolling crowd on the wooden sidewalk that bordered the square.

That he was a cowboy fresh off the range was very apparent to the townsmen, who smiled knowingly as Billy walked stiffly in his brand new clothes, clutching a cigar to which he was unaccustomed. A shipping point for cattle, the town had seen countless such cowboys as him, who recklessly spent their hard-earned wages in a vain attempt at looking like the town dwellers.

To the uncomprehending Billy, however, the smiles directed at him by the townsmen seemed the gestures of a friendly people.

It was after dark when Billy entered the Tivoli Hotel dining room and was seated by a somber waiter wearing a red swallow-tailed coat. Another waiter brought him the menu, and yet another took his order. Back in Sayers Flat, in the small restaurant where he usually ate when in town, the cook did it all, including washing the dishes. He was bewildered by all the attention shown him by the large dining staff, who were dressed better even than the circuit rider who made his rounds to the Rocking J.

Feeling the weight of the gold coins in his pockets, he suddenly felt his confidence returning, knowing that, with Mr. Sanderson's money, he had no reason to be intimidated by the fancy, obsequious waiters. Finally at ease in his situation, he snapped his fingers for the waiters, following the custom he had noted of the other patrons of the dining room.

Ordering exotic dishes that he had only heard about, Billy did himself proud, and was so stuffed by he time the dessert cart came to his table that he had to apologize to the crest-fallen dessert waiter.

In his room, Billy undressed and folded his new outfit across a chair, climbing into the huge bed. He was not accustomed to the softness of the down mattress, and sleep would not come. So soft was his bed that his weight had made a furrow that conformed to his body and made it difficult for him to roll over or even change position.

For what seemed like hours he tossed fitfully, praying for sleep that would not come. Finally, in a last-ditch effort to find the rest he so needed, he pulled the blankets from the bed and made them into a pallet much like his familiar bedroll, and was soon fast asleep.

At mid-morning Billy made his way through a large, milling crowd at the train depot. With dozens of wagons and horses tied to the hitching rails, he found it difficult to park the buckboard, and had to go much beyond the station and walk back.

A couple of hundred jubilant people were standing around the depot in anticipation of the arrival of the scheduled westbound train, and judging by the large banner Billy saw displayed over the station platform, the crowd was awaiting the arrival of Miss Jenny Lind, The Swedish Nightingale, who, although advanced in age, was still a drawing card wherever she performed.

"Say, young fellow," an old man said, grabbing Billy by his arm, "would ye be going to the opry house to see Miss Jenny whilst she's in town? Me, I got myself tickets for all her performances, smack dab in the front row."

"I haven't thought on it, mister. I'm not very familiar with Miss Lind," Billy said, trying to tear himself away from the man.

"Not familiar with Miss Jenny? Why, I seen her twenty year ago up in Denver, Colorady, and such a beauty you wouldn't believe—and a voice like a angel—you ast me."

Billy finally managed to tear himself away from the exuberant old man and walked among the crowd, finding himself caught up in the spirit of the occasion. On the station platform a bandstand had been erected, and a brass band was playing an off-key rendition of "Camptown Races." In the center of the platform a pompous-looking man who had all the appearances of a political official was arranging a nervous group of bouquet-carrying children dressed in white, and all about the depot small boys set off firecrackers.

Above all the combined noises of the crowd, the whistle

of the approaching train could be heard as it made its way through the endless rows of cattle pens that lined the tracks.

Billy made his way to the outside of the crowd and waited. Despite what the ranch owner had told him, he still had no idea how he was to recognize the Sanderson ladies, particularly with half the town jamming the depot. He would follow Mr. Sanderson's instructions and look for a fancy black horse. When he found the horse, he assumed, he would also find the ladies.

As the train hissed to a stop in front of the station platform, the band began to play a raucous tune, a string of firecrackers began exploding, and the crowd began cheering wildly.

Making his way around the jubilant crowd to the cattle-holding pens on the opposite side of the station, Billy saw several men placing a loading ramp in position in front of a stock car. When the ramp was in place, a beautiful girl in tight denims entered the car and returned, leading a horse like none he had ever seen.

He could not decide who had the better lines, the girl or the horse. Although smaller than expected, the Arabian had well-formed shoulders and a long, graceful neck that supported an exceptionally beautiful head, and Billy could not help thinking that the same description fit the girl who was holding its lead rope; she was equally graceful and sleek, and he judged her to be about seventeen or eighteen years old, with long blonde hair and a perfect figure. Somehow it just seemed natural to Billy that she was the one to lead the regal animal from the train.

The horse appeared skittish, however, and the girl was having a time of it trying to calm him down. Thinking he had better introduce himself right away and offer her some assistance with the nervous animal, Billy made his way through the small circle of gawkers and idlers and approached the girl.

By the time he had made his way to the base of the loading platform, the horse was somewhat calmer. Yet it was apparent to Billy that he was still a little jittery and disoriented.

"Excuse me, ma'am," Billy drawled, removing his hat, "would you by chance be Miss Sanderson?"

"What if I am? Am I supposed to know you, cowboy?"

"I'm Billy Bayes, ma'am. Your pa sent me to accompany you ladies and the horse to the Rocking J. He would've come himself, but his gout got to acting up on him again."

"It's sufficient only to say my father sent you, Mr. Bayes. I'm certain he wouldn't want the state of his health announced in public."

"Yes, of course. Sorry, ma'am. Would you like for me to take the horse off your hands now?"

As the girl reached to hand Billy the Arabian's lead rope, a string of firecrackers began exploding underneath the cattle car behind them, causing the nervous horse to rear, jerking free from the hands of the surprised girl. Coming down on all four feet, he immediately bolted through the circle of scattering onlookers and galloped across the rail yard toward the open foothills.

For a long moment there was only stunned silence, then one of the onlookers said, "Would you just look at that sucker run. I ain't never seen nothing like it. He's gone!"

"You . . . you . . . just look what you did!" the girl cried, turning on Billy accusingly. "You've lost my father's horse."

"Me? I didn't do anything. He must've spooked."

"It was your fault for distracting me. I had him in perfect control until you interfered. Oh, my father will be simply furious if we lose that horse. You've got to get him back—right away.''

''I drove the buckboard to the station, ma'am. My horse is stabled behind the Tivoli Hotel, and I expect it'll take some time to make my way there and throw a saddle on him.''

''Then get your horse by all means, Mr. Bayes. Our bags are there on the loading platform,'' she said, pointing with her quirt.

''Getting the buckboard to the platform and loading your bags is only going to slow me down, ma'am. I'll just point it out to you, then trot up to the livery and saddle my horse. I think it probably best you ladies get yourselves to the hotel.''

''Young man,'' said an older woman nearby, ''I am Effie Sanderson, and I do not believe it would go well for you when I tell my brother how you left two defenseless ladies stranded at the train depot. I must insist that you load our luggage at once and get us to our hotel. You may go after the horse after seeing to our comfort. Do I make myself perfectly clear on that, sir?''

''Whatever you say, ma'am.''

Billy brought the buckboard to the station platform and loaded the ladies' trunks and valises. By now the older woman was leaning against the building with her eyes tightly closed and clutching her chest with her arms. ''Is she all right?'' Billy asked the girl.

''She most certainly is not all right, and neither am I, for that matter. We are both concerned about the Arabian. My father entrusted his safe delivery to us, and you've lost him.''

''You're not still blaming that on *me*? I don't think it

was anybody's fault—unless it was those kids with the fireworks.''

''Perhaps so, Mr. Bayes, if you wish to place the blame
on someone else in order to clear yourself of the responsibility for having lost him. Regardless of who is to blame,
my aunt and I will be unable to rest until he's recovered,''
she said, flashing her green eyes in defiance as she braced
herself for Billy's response.

But having learned the stubborn ways of women while
living with his six female cousins back on his uncle's farm,
Billy knew that any further argument with the girl was
tantamount to taking a sidewinder by the tail. ''I'll find that
horse and bring it back to town, ma'am. You can be dang
sure of that.''

''As for me I shall have to be convinced of that, young
man,'' said the older woman. ''If you are quite finished
patting yourself on the back, you may assist me aboard the
wagon, if you please.''

After helping Effie Sanderson onto the high seat of the
buckboard, he reached out to take the hand of her niece,
only to have her brush it aside and climb onto the wagon
unassisted.

Taking the reins, the girl said, ''We'll drop you off at
the livery, Mr. Bayes, and have the hotel porter handle the
disposition of our luggage and the buckboard. I should think
you'll be quite busy enough chasing after the Arabian.''

''Whatever you say, ma'am.''

''And we don't wish to see you back in town until that
horse is safely stalled in the livery.''

''Yes, ma'am.''

Now, if that don't top all, Billy said to himself, cinching
his saddle on the chestnut. That dang-blasted, high-strung
female is blaming me for the loss of that infernal fancy

horse. If I don't come back with him, I might as well keep right on riding. She really has herself convinced that I'm the one who caused him to bolt, and she'll probably convince her pa as well. Women.

But son-of-a-gun, he mused, she's a pretty little vixen—even when she's angry. Too bad she's a spoiled brat. Still . . . The very thought of the girl living at the Rocking J filled him with excitement. Living in that close proximity, their paths would surely have to cross often. No way to avoid it, he thought happily.

He knew all about girls like Rebecca Sanderson; he had seen too many like her in Sayers Flat, the spoiled daughters of wealthy ranchers, with their back-East, finishing school manners and their snobbish attitudes, fancy girls who wouldn't give an ordinary cowboy the time of day.

Well, he would just show *her* the stuff Bill Bayes was made of—if he had to chase that fool horse to Santa Fe and back again. Why, he would ride into Bent Rock and place the Arabian's lead rope in her hand and let her know just who she was dealing with.

Billy had no idea of the length of time it would take to track down the horse and capture him, but he was much too experienced with the unpredictability of the mountainous countryside to venture out without the provisions necessary for an extended stay.

Stopping at a general store as he was leaving town, he purchased a slab of bacon, a poke of flour, and a bag of coffee. As an afterthought he added a box of .44-40 cartridges for his six-gun and rifle.

Chapter 4

By the time Billy's preparations were completed and he had taken up the Arabian's trail outside of town it was nearing the noon hour. Not having eaten since the night before, his stomach was growling, but he dared not take the time to eat. Once he had the Arabian's lead rope fastened to his saddle horn, or whenever it turned dark, he would eat, but not before.

It didn't take an expert to determine that the elusive Arabian was heading for the high country, and Billy noticed right off that its hoof marks were discernible among the other tracks in the area, making his job of trailing him just that much easier.

And it was a fair assumption that the liberated horse could run until he either tired or found good grazing. With the spring growth of grass in the foothills, the horse would most likely find himself a good patch of grass and stay put for a spell.

If his hunch proved correct, Billy had little reason to doubt that he would be back at the hotel by dark, the Arabian safely stalled in the livery, and himself cutting into a thick, juicy steak.

For nearly an hour Billy tracked the Arabian before the signs indicated he had slowed from a leisurely jog to an ambling walk. And it was just as he had figured. The horse was now wandering about aimlessly while grazing on patches of sparse grass. Farther along, he found signs that he had stopped to drink from a running stream and rested before moving on.

Now at a higher elevation, Billy tracked the horse through a narrow defile and lost his trail on the rocky ground on the opposite side of the passage. An entire hour was lost as he circled and backtracked to again pick up the horse's tracks.

Time was against him now if he expected to catch the horse and return to Bent Rock before dark. Nervously, Billy looked at the sun teetering on the western horizon, and swore softly to himself. The thing was hardly going the way he had planned it, and he resigned himself to the fact he would be spending the night on the trail, even if he did manage to catch the Arabian before dark set in.

It was twilight when Billy finally came upon the horse. Grazing on a grassy slope near a cottonwood-bordered stream, he did not shy from the kid when he dismounted and took his lead rope.

"Well, old son, you're quite the troublemaker, you know. But I have to hand you one thing, you certainly can pick a campsite. I couldn't have found a better spot to bed down for the night if I had been looking for it on purpose," Billy said, talking soothingly to the Arabian while rubbing his neck with his free hand.

"As soon as I water my chestnut, I'm going to tether you two cayuses on this knoll and dig myself in for the night next to that creek. And if hell freezes over I'm going to have myself some grub and some sleep. You two got that?"

Soon, darkness came to shrink the space around him, and Billy finished a meal of bacon and slipjacks cooked over an open fire, relaxing with a steaming cup of coffee. Sitting close to the fire with a blanket wrapped around him, his thoughts again returned to the beautiful green-eyed girl back in town. As much as he detested girls of her class, he could not shake her from his mind, and in spite of their obvious differences, he felt that underneath her attitude toward him earlier in the day, there existed between them a mutual attraction. How he knew that to be a fact he hadn't the foggiest notion, but he just did.

That she was part hellcat was already apparent to him, but maybe she would react differently toward him when he came riding into town with the Arabian stallion in tow. After all, he reasoned, it was the Arabian that started them off on the wrong foot, so why not the return of the animal to soften her attitude.

After making a final check of the horses, Billy gathered a pile of juniper boughs from the trees that grew profusely along the knoll and carried them to the camp for cushioning his bedroll. As was his habit when sleeping on the trail, he removed his six-gun from its holster and placed it within reach when he retired for the night.

"*Hombre.*"

The voice came to Billy as if through a dense fog, persistent and heavily accented, and was followed by a nudge to his ribs.

"*Hombre,*" repeated the voice, followed by even a harder nudge to his ribcage. "Wake up, *hombre.*"

Slowly opening his eyes, Billy found himself face to face with what had to be the ugliest Mexican he had ever seen. His bad breath alone was enough to cause him to realize he wasn't dreaming the man.

As Billy circumspectly felt for his six-gun, the Mexican laughed, exposing missing and yellow teeth, and said, "You are maybe looking for this gun?" He then pulled back the hammer and pressed the barrel against Billy's nose.

"*Señor*," Billy whispered hoarsely, "that gun has a very fickle trigger. Would you please not point it at me? It has a bad habit of firing accidentally when it's cocked."

"I will release the hammer only, but you must not be so foolish as to make me shoot you, okay?"

"I won't move the first muscle, I swear."

"This *pistola*, it is a very beautiful weapon, *hombre*. But tell me, how is it that such a young boy as yourself can afford such a gun? I think I would like to have it."

"By all means take it. It's yours."

"*Si*, I think so too."

Another Mexican, somewhat taller and thinner than the one holding the gun on Billy, stepped from the early-morning shadows and tossed a few sticks of wood on the hot coals of the campfire. Catching sight of the gun in his partner's hand he said, "That is a very beautiful *pistola*, cousin."

"*Si*," he said proudly, waving the six-gun to test the feel of it in his hand, "it is mine. This *gringo* made me a present of it."

"Ah, Luis, I would give my *cajones* for such a *pistola* as that one."

"But Pancho, already I have let you keep the *gringo's* rifle. Why must you always be so greedy? The *pistola* is mine to keep."

"If you say, cousin."

"I say. And the horse. Did I not let you keep the *gringo's* chestnut horse."

"*Si*, Cousin, you did allow me to take the chestnut horse, but I much prefer the black one. *Ching' su madre*, I have never seen such a horse. I would give my *cajones* for such a *caballo*."

"Pancho, Pancho, Pancho, my dear sweet cousin, what-

ever am I going to do with you? To every man there is
given *cajones*, and already this day you have wished to
exchange yours for a horse and a gun. Think about that,
cousin, your *cajones.* . . .

"You are yet a young man, Pancho, and perhaps you
will someday marry a beautiful *señorita* and have need of
your *cajones* with which to make many sons. So why is it
you wish to exchange them for horses and guns—a horse
that will someday die, and a gun that men will attempt to
steal from you out of envy. No, my *compañero*, you must
take your *cajones* very seriously."

"I only make a little joke, Luis. It is my way, as you,
my own cousin, should know."

"But a man does not make such a joke about his *cajones*.
It is a very serious matter, a man's *cajones*."

"But still, I would like to have the black horse for myself," the thin Mexican said demandingly, swinging Billy's
rifle from behind his back where he had it concealed.

Leveling the six-gun with the hair trigger, the squatting
bandit got off two quick rounds before the rifle could be
aimed, and the thin Mexican collapsed onto the campfire,
blood spouting from his throat.

Walking over to the dying bandit, the one called Luis
rolled him from the fire with the toe of his *huaraches* and
said, "Oh, Pancho, my dear sweet cousin, why did you
have to be so greedy? How will I ever explain to my father's
sister that her only son is dead? Poor Pancho, you could
have had the beautiful chestnut horse and the *gringo's* rifle.
Now you have nothing."

Holding his breath, Billy tried to make himself small. If
the man was in a killing mood—which he hoped he wasn't—
he could find himself joining the bandit who was gurgling
his last breath beside the fire.

"*Hombre,*" he said, turning on Billy, "you will give me your money now, for I wish to be on my way to Mexico."

Billy did not hesitate to hand the bandit the pouch containing the gold; he had quickly concluded that any man who would shoot down his own cousin over trifles would likely do no less to a perfect stranger.

Taking the gold and appraising the weight of it in his palm, the bandit said, "Ah, but I am a poor man—so very poor that you would not understand. And you, still just a boy and you have so very much. I think tomorrow . . . maybe next week, you will again buy a horse and gun. *Si,* for you *gringos* it is an easy thing to do. But for me, a *peon,* I can only take from you what is not available to me in my country."

"But the black horse, *señor,*" Billy pleaded, "is not mine, and I cannot return without him. Please, take everything I have except for that horse."

"Ahh, I am sorry for you, *hombre.* As I say, I am but a poor Mexican, *si,* but I am not stupid about horses. That is one magnificent animal, the black horse. If I take him to Mexico I can sell him for much gold to one of the rich *haciendas.* And from the money I will get for the horse I can have many beautiful *señoritas* and never work again. Oh, but you just do not understand, *hombre.*"

"But I am responsible for that horse, *señor.* I will lose my job if I return without him."

"*Hombre, hombre.* I give you your life, and is that not a precious thing I give you? *Si,* it is true. I will not kill you as you may think, but that man," he said, pointing to the dead bandit sadly, "the son of my father's sister, was not a good man. He would kill his very own cousin for a horse. I killed him only that I might live. You yourself saw that.

I am a thief, that is true, but I do not kill a man without cause.

"I will also take your rifle, *hombre*," he said, picking up the weapon where the dead bandit had dropped it. "Such a weapon can shoot a man in the back from a great distance, and I do not wish to be shot in the back. *Adios, hombre*."

Billy watched helplessly as the bandit released a saddled mule and waved it off with his *sombrero*. The liberated mule, which ran like a horse, headed into the nearby hills at a gallop, and was soon lost in the shadows.

Mounting a dun pony, the bandit then saluted Billy and rode south, leading the chestnut and Arabian. Flinging his hat to the ground, Billy stood watching in disbelief as the bandit and the horses disappeared over a distant rise.

In the awakening dawn, Billy began walking in the direction he had last seen the fleeing mule. He at once realized, however, that it was going to be difficult to follow the tracks of the unshod mule over the rocky terrain, and began to lose valuable time in having to circle and backtrack.

It appeared to Billy that the mule was wandering aimlessly through the piñons and cedars, stopping often to graze before moving on again, and several times he found himself crossing his previous trails, causing him to conclude that he was wasting his time by trying to catch the animal without some sort of plan.

Figuring himself to be smarter than any mule alive, Billy decided to climb to a higher elevation and watch for the animal over a broader area. It was now apparent to him that the mule was remaining in the approximate vicinity, and all he had to do was wait him out. Eventually, he would have to expose himself in his wanderings.

* * *

At the Tivoli Hotel back in Bent Rock, the two Sanderson women were finishing a late breakfast in the hotel's adjoining dining room. They were having their coffee and discussing local fashions when Becky broached the subject of the missing Arabian. Since the horse had bolted to freedom, little mention of it had been made in their conversations, both women feeling secure in their assumptions that the young ranch hand would eventually track down the horse and return with him to town.

"I checked with the desk this morning, Auntie, and it seems our Mr. Bayes didn't return to his room last night. I fear all didn't go well with him. Surely he should've caught the Arabian long before now, wouldn't you think?"

"I would certainly think so. I must admit that I have also been worried about the situation. Mr. Bayes does appear such a young man to be chasing around this wild country by himself. I hope he has not put himself in some sort of danger because of that horse—although the safe return of the Arabian is my main concern."

"Oh, I'm certain Mr. Bayes knows his business, Auntie, or else Father wouldn't have sent him to meet us. With the number of experienced older hands on the Rocking J, father would not have sent someone who he did not believe capable of seeing us safely to the ranch. In that I know Father only too well."

"Now that the subject is open, I have to confess that I also checked with the desk this morning. My feeling is that our Mr. Bayes found himself too far distant from the town when he captured the horse, and decided to spend the night out there somewhere—at least I hope the situation is no worse than that."

Becky hardly seemed to hear her aunt's words as she stared vacantly at the early crowd already parading past the fly-specked window where they sat. "You know, I feel a little guilty about the way I lashed out at him yesterday. That expression on his face . . . "

"Yes, I have hesitated to bring it up, dear, but I do feel that you are the one, after all, who is responsible for his being out there chasing after the Arabian. And you were a little harsh with him."

"I must confess I did come on a bit strong, Auntie."

"Strong is not the word for it. Why, you actually accused the young man of losing the horse, and we both know it was not the case at at all. It was only through a combination of circumstances that the Arabian bolted, and I suppose if the blame should be placed on any one thing in particular, it would have to be those infernal fireworks. You blatantly accused the young man of losing the horse, and he was nearly beside himself. Why, I could see it in his eyes— even from where I stood watching."

Becky laughed impishly. "I knew it wasn't his fault, Auntie, and he knew it as well. But you have to understand the ego of young men like Mr. Bayes. They're awfully full of themselves at his age—and so easily intimidated by a pretty face. If Mr. Bayes thinks I hold him responsible for the loss of the Arabian, he'll go to any extreme to exonerate himself. I realize I have been gone from the ranch for a good number of years, but I still remember how those young cowboys think; they would rather be anything than wrong."

"Dear me, child, young ladies these days are so shamelessly guileful—not at all like when I was your age. That poor, unsuspecting young man. You really should be ashamed of yourself, Rebecca."

"Well, I am—just a little. That dumbfounded look on his face when I accused him of losing the horse. And ordering him not to return to town without it. I worried about it all night.''

''I suppose a little remorse is better than none at all, but do try and make it up to him when he returns—if he returns.''

Becky rested her chin on her interlaced fingers and looked off into space. Shortly, focusing on her aunt, she said, ''Don't you think, Auntie, that he—Mr. Bayes—is awfully handsome?''

''My gracious, Rebecca, remember who you are, child. Why, when I think of all the money your poor father has spent in making a lady of you—I hope all those years at the best finishing school in Baltimore have not been a complete waste.''

''I only said he was handsome, Auntie. It doesn't take an education to see *that*.''

''That is true enough, but ladies of breeding do not discuss such things so openly. But since you brought it up,'' she said, lowering her voice to a near whisper, ''I think he is extremely handsome—in an animal sort of way. Why, if only I were a young girl again—''

''Auntie!'' Becky exclaimed, color rising to her face.

''Oh come, child, do not act so shocked. You asked for my opinion and I gave it. So there.''

''Yes, of course, Auntie. It's just that I never expected such frankness coming from you.''

''But do let us change the subject, Rebecca. We have a week yet to spend in Bent Rock, and Jenny Lind is appearing here for a few days. Why don't we make plans to see her show.''

''I would love to see her show, Auntie, especially after meeting her on the train. But I'm so terribly worried about the Arabian. What will we do if Mr. Bayes doesn't return to Bent Rock with the horse? You know . . . if something happened to him out there?''

''The thought has occurred to me that Mr. Bayes might not return, but do let us cross that bridge when we come to it. Besides, I have the feeling that he is much more capable than we give him credit. You said it yourself, why else would your father have sent him to see us to the Rocking J?''

Chapter 5

The sun fully up, Billy maintained his perch at an elevation that afforded him a wide view of the area in which he had earlier lost the trail of the mule. For over an hour he had scanned the opposite treeline, looking for movement, and felt he was no closer to spotting the elusive animal than when he had started.

He could only worry that while he lost precious time waiting for the mule to make his appearance, the Arabian was that much closer to the border, and oblivion. He rolled another smoke and continued watching the area about him. It was while he cupped the match to his cigarette that he thought he saw a movement in the pine and cedar thicket down the slope from where he waited. Then he saw it again, a movement so slight that it could have been made by a bird flitting through the tree boughs.

He kept his eyes trained to the point where he had seen the movement, and moments later it appeared that an entire tree was in motion. Stamping out the cigarette, he quickly ran down the slope and across a clearing to the opposite treeline.

Billy could not believe his good luck. The mule's rein was caught in the forks of a low-growing pine limb, holding him a captive. "Well, mule, I sure hope you had yourself a good rest while you were all tangled up here, because this son is going to give you some English lessons soon as I free you," Billy said laughingly.

Leading the docile animal to an opening in the thick growth, Billy then climbed into the derelict saddle and rode him into the camp. Time was against him if he expected to catch the bandit before he crossed the border into Mexico, and he hadn't a moment to lose.

At the edge of the camp, Billy removed the Mexican's worn saddle and replaced it with his own, then he gathered his warbag, bedroll, and coffee pot and secured them for traveling. After filling his canteen from the creek, he pointed the mule south.

Billy felt badly about leaving the dead bandit unburied back at the camp, but he had neither a shovel with which to dig a hole nor the time in which to gather rocks from the surrounding hills to shield his remains from predators. Already he could see several vultures riding the updrafts, seeking the source of death.

That the bandit was heading straightaway for the border with the horses was now confirmed in Billy's mind by the southerly route that he was traveling. That in itself made tracking him that much easier; whenever the hoofprints were lost over rocky ground, Billy merely continued south until the rough ground ended and the tracks took up again.

The way Billy had it figured, the bandit either thought he would be unable to catch the mule and follow after him, or else thought a man without a gun posed no serious threat. But no matter what his reason, he made no apparent effort to disguise his trail.

Billy couldn't believe the way things had been going for him since he first laid eyes on the Arabian. He knew, without a doubt, that he was in no way responsible for the initial loss of the horse, even when that hot-tempered Sanderson chit claimed differently.

Losing the Arabian to the Mexican bandit was an altogether different matter; that was clearly his fault and he wouldn't deny it. He had let his guard down, and deserved what he got. He was much too trail-wise to sleep in the open without taking steps to protect himself, and he was now paying the price for his carelessness.

What would old Josh think if he came dragging back to the Rocking J without the Arabian? Without his horse and guns? Worse still, what would Paul Sanderson think? The questions he posed to himself were ones he did not wish to dwell on; if he were to catch up with the bandit and retrieve all that was taken from him—and he was determined to do that very thing, regardless of the hardships and risks to himself—the questions would then be moot ones.

And, although Billy had openly admitted it to himself from the very beginning, he wanted to capture the Arabian in order that he might win Becky Sanderson's approval. He wanted to impress her in the only way he knew how.

The cedars and piñons of the foothills soon gave way to the sagebrush of the flat country, and Billy could see for miles across the vast open land that lay before him. Wiping his perspiring brow, he swore softly to himself and spurred the hardy mule on. Although he had never traveled this particular part of the country, he knew from having heard others speak of it that it was a rough, dry land he was entering, and that water in these parts was scarce to non-existent.

Having earlier filled his canteen at the camp, Billy wasn't too concerned about water quite yet, but not knowing what conditions awaited him he conserved his diminishing supply by going longer without touching his canteen, and taking only small sips when he did so.

The bandit had to know the country through which Billy was tracking him, he figured, but he could not have been any better provided than he was, which in itself gave him cause to believe that the man knew of a source of water within the range of travel. For Billy, there was solace in the thought that water would be there for him before the need of it would become too critical.

In the late afternoon, in a little cantina in a remote village situated near the Pecos, three tough-looking Americans sat idly around a table drinking watered *pulque* and playing cards. They were the remnants of a once-notorious gang of outlaws who called themselves the Brogen Gang. In their more active outlaw years, their name alone struck terror in the hearts of bank tellers and stage drivers and train engineers from Amarillo in the Texas panhandle to Albuquerque. No organized gang of thieves in the entire history of that area of the West had been so successful in their craft, and yet they had managed to elude any and all who thought to capture them.

But that was then. Now relics of an era when there was little to no law in the West, the three remaining members of the depleted gang led a nomadic existence, still running from a law that no longer actively chased after them, or, for that matter, even remembered who they were.

Brogen was a huge man, impressive in both his build and his carriage, even now in his middling age, and his full beard and his unkempt hair had long since turned gray with age, his small, obsidian eyes those of a hunted man, darting, always taking in his surroundings.

Fisk, whose short stocky body had given way to flab,

was a pseudo-intellectual who had earlier made his living by teaching secondary students at an exclusive girl's school in New York City. Rumor had it that he was caught having an illicit affair with one of his young charges, the daughter of a wealthy entrepreneur, and he had narrowly escaped being shot by the irate father by fleeing west.

Beak, whose prominent nose was the source of his nickname, was the youngest member of the gang, and also the smallest. Lightning fast with his pair of six-guns as a youngster, age had done little to diminish his skill in that area, and his deadly accuracy at hitting the target at which he aimed was no less equal to the impressive speed of his draw.

As is the nature of some pint-sized men, Beak was quick to take offense at any remark made in reference to his diminutive stature, and any man who had been so foolish as to underestimate the little man's ability to react to any such remark never lived long enough to regret his error in judgement.

It was Brogen, the ever-vigilant leader of the outlaw gang, who first heard the horses as they entered the village. "Sounds like company," he said, his gravelly voice breaking the stillness of the near-empty cantina.

Beak studied the cards in his hands and nodded disinterestedly. He had long since grown accustomed to his leaders's nervous habit of thinking every sound he heard was that of a posse riding in pursuit. "Sure it ain't your nerves again, boss? I don't hear nothing."

"Then you're going deaf with age. I guess I know the sounds of horses when I hear 'em," Brogen growled.

Fisk tossed in his hand and strained to listen. "You're right. I hear something. In fact, I hear several horses, and they seem to be heading this way. Why don't you check it out, Beak."

"Why the deuce should I be the one to check it out. Why don't you check it out your own dang self?"

"Because you're closer to the door, that's why."

"Hell fire, you tub of lard, I'm sitting right here beside you."

"True enough, but you're still the closest to the door."

"Beak do this, Beak do that. I thought we was equal partners."

"If it's too much bother for you two lazy varmints, I'll check it out myself. It could be a posse for all you care." Brogen said, glaring at the two arguing outlaws.

"I kinda wish it was a posse," Beak mused. "I ain't had one chasing me fer so long, I'm beginning to feel slighted."

Brogen looked at the little man in exasperation, then stiffly raised his large frame and walked to the batwing doors and peered out over them, keeping himself in the shadows. "Well, partners, come look what that bean-eater, Luis, done stole himself," Brogen said excitedly.

Overcome with curiosity, the others raised themselves and looked out over the batwings.

"My oh my, that is one fine-looking animal. I wonder who he had to kill to get a horse like that?" Beak said.

Brogen wiped his mouth with his sleeve and said, "Ast him your own self, why don't you. Appears he's headed for the cantina. Now sit down and act natural, both of you. Ain't no need in spooking him by gawking like this."

After watering the horses at a nearby trough, the Mexican bandit led them to the cantina and tied them to the hitching rail. Turning a complete circle and checking out the surrounding area, he then started for the cantina door.

Inside, the three outlaws pretended to play cards, waiting for the Mexican to enter, but already their minds were at work, wondering how big a price the black horse would bring when they took it from the Mexican and sold it to someone who knew its value. Like the bandit, the outlaws were not ignorant of its probable fine blood.

The Mexican sauntered into the cantina and stood momentarily as his eyes adjusted to the dark interior. When he recognized the three American outlaws sitting at the front table, he appeared hesitant.

"Why, hello there, *amigo*," Brogen hailed in a loud voice. "Take a chair and have a drink with your old *compadres*, why don't you."

An almost imperceptible expression of fear and suspicion crossed the bandit's face, but he managed to maintain his composure as he joined the three outlaws at their table. Yet his movements were guarded as he took the offered chair and seated himself.

"*Señor* Brogen, how are you my friend? Last year in El Paso I heard the rumor that you were dead. It is good to see it is not so."

"Well, I'm here to tell you it ain't so. How is it with you, Luis? Still running those Mexican scrubs across the border?"

"Not so much since I last saw you. It is a very bad time for honest businessmen like myself. *Federales* watch the border closely now, and they demand their cut of everything that crosses. They are so very greedy that I am left with nothing. And yourself, *amigo*, you are doing well these days?"

"Oh, we're doing pretty good for ourselves, my partners and me—ain't we fellows?"

"Hell yeah," Beak said sarcastically. "We're rolling in it."

"Splendidly," Fisk added. "In fact, I'm thinking of

opening my own bank, just to have a place to store all the extra money.''

"It is good you are doing so well, *señors*. But me, *ching' su madre*, I am so poor.''

"Oh, I don't know about that, Luis. Those are some fine-looking cayuses you're leading around, especially the black one. Seems to me like you're doing pretty good for a poor man,'' Brogen said, grinning through his beard.

"*Señor* Brogen, did I not tell you? The times are so hard for me that I am forced to work for wages . . . I am delivering these horses to a rich *hacienda* in Chihuahua. The pay, it is not so good, to be sure, but a man must make a living, you understand.''

"I only understand one thing, Luis. The day that Luis Alvarez does an honest day's work, it's time for even the likes of me to hang it up. Who you trying to kid, anyhow? This is your old friend Brogen you're talking to, *compadre*.''

"But it is true, *amigo*. *Si*, I am forced to do this thing to put food on my table. It is a very sad thing, is it not, when a great *bandido* like myself has to turn to honest work to provide for himself?''

"Sure, *compadre*, it is a very sad thing, indeed. You got our sympathy, don't he fellows?''

"He's got mine,'' Beak said with a wink.

Brogen leaned toward the Mexican and lowered his voice confidentially and said, "Tell me, Luis, just who the hell you delivering those horses for?''

"Who? Why, that would be . . . ah . . . Don Angel—Si, Don Angel Dominguez. Don Angel Dominguez wishes to be rid of these horses, so he has me to deliver them to his friend in Mexico.''

"You don't say? Would that be the same Don Angel who

has the big *hacienda* up near Las Vegas?'' Brogen baited him.

"*Si*, the very same, *amigo*! You know of him, Don Angel?''

"Why, I reckon I do. Hell, everybody in these parts knows about Don Angel, the richest man in the entire territory. But tell me, Luis, when was the last time you saw this Don Angel?''

"When? When did I last see him? Ahh . . . last night. *Si*. It was only last night when he asked me to deliver these horses to his friend in Chihuahua. *Si*, only last night it was.''

Brogen shook his head ''no'' several times and looked at the bandit disapprovingly. ''Now that's mighty peculiar, *Amigo*. You see, Don Angel Dominguez died a few months back, and I hear it that a wealthy Englishman is dickering with his widow to buy his spread—lock, stock, and barrel. Now, just how do you explain that?''

"*Ching' su madre*! Did I say Don Angel? It must be the hot sun on my head. I meant to say Don . . . ah. . . . Oh, is it so late already, *señors*? I must leave right away. You see, I have ten *compadres* waiting for me just outside of this village, and they will be sure to worry and come looking for me, I think.''

"You don't have to be in such a hurry to go, *amigo*. Have another drink with us before you leave,'' Brogen said with a wide grin.

"Thank you, but my *compadres* wait for me, and I do not wish for them to worry and come looking for me. Thank you again for the *pulque* . . . *adios*.''

After the Mexican had made a fast exit from the town, Brogen broke into laughter, slapping his knees. "Delivering them to Don Angel,'' he said mockingly between fits of laughter. "Why, that damn greaser done stole them horses sure as shooting."

"I didn't know Don Angel died," Beak said thoughtfully.

"He didn't, you idjit. That Mexican didn't know it either. I made up that part just to test him."

"Then how did he come by them fancy horses?"

"I'm not sure, but I got an idee he stole them from the Rocking J spread."

"From Sanderson? Why do you suspect that?" Fisk asked.

"Simple. The brand on that chestnut. I notice things like that, you see. The black wasn't showing a brand, but my guess is they both come from the Rocking J, what with Sanderson being into horse-breeding of late."

"A horse like that black would be worth a lot of money in Mexico, I'll bet. There ain't nothing those rich dons like better than strutting around on a fancy horse," Beak said.

"It should be worth as much to Sanderson, and we don't have to go all the way to Mexico to collect," Brogen said slyly.

"And just how do you propose to accomplish that?" Fisk asked.

"Ransom."

"Ransom?"

"Why not. When we take him from that greaser, we'll hold him in that old hideout up near Rociada and send Sanderson a ransom note."

Fisk drummed his fingers on the table as he thought over the plan. "It just might work," he agreed. "If not, we still have the alternative of taking him to Mexico as a last resort."

Beak removed his six-guns, checked the loads, and slid

them back into their holsters and said, "You think that greaser's had enough lead on us."

"Yeah, by the time we saddle up he should be far enough along the trail."

"What about the ten friends he claimed to have waiting for him? If he wasn't lying, they would have us outnumbered by more than three to one. I don't think we can handle that sort of odds."

"He was bluffing. He didn't like the odds he saw here, so he made up some of his own," Brogen said with a laugh. "All those *bandidos* are the same. They're only tough when they figure they have the advantage. Stand up to them and they run like rabbits.

"He's heading for the border, without a doubt, and I figure he'll get just far enough out of town to make certain he wasn't followed before he camps for the night. We'll take him then."

Chapter 6

T he sun had already slid out of sight over the distant
hills, and the western horizon was a blaze of rapidly shifting
colors as Billy rode into the little adobe village. He saw no
more than a dozen squalid dwellings scattered along the
dusty trail, and a few dark-skinned, half-naked children and
mangy dogs running about.

He drew up the mule and studied the immediate area. On
the far side of the village was a small cantina, with a corral
of sorts attached to the rear, and Billy could see that the
bandit's trail headed in that direction, but he wasn't at all
certain whether the man was still in the building or had only
rested there before continuing on.

Swinging sharply to the bank of the Pecos, Billy kept the
cottonwoods between himself and the village as he circled
behind the corral and verified that the horses were not there.

Dismounting, he led the mule around the cantina and tied
him to the hitching rail, studying the many fresh tracks
leading south out of town. He was uneasy about the several
sets of tracks that covered those of the bandit's. Maybe it
was only coincidental that the three sets of tracks followed
the bandit out of the village, but if the men who were riding
the horses were friends of the bandit, Billy had to know
what he was up against. He hadn't counted on the new odds,
and found the thought unsettling.

Entering the cantina, Billy found it empty except for a

56

middle-aged, overweight woman who looked at him without interest from behind the bar. Greeting him with only a nod of her head, she placed a bottle in front of him and said, "You would like some *pulque*, maybe?"

"No, thank you, *señora*. I'm looking for someone—a heavy-set Mexican who was traveling through here with a couple of horses. His tracks indicate he tied off in front of this building."

The woman, who could have been very beautiful, Billy thought, except for a badly pock-marked face that indicated a bout with smallpox in her past, smiled at him and said, "Ah, it is really the horses you are interested in, is that not so? The man you speak of is a *bandido*, but you must know that already. *Si*, I know of the man you seek. I know everything that happens in this village."

"Then would you mind telling me how long it's been since he rode out?"

"*Si*, I could. But you must understand, *señor*, this small village is very, very poor. In this village, if I do something for you, then you must do something for me in return. It is our way of surviving. I know much important information which might be of interest to you. *Comprende*?"

Billy searched through his pockets and retrieved a loose gold coin that had been overlooked by the bandit earlier. Placing his hand over the five-dollar coin on the counter in front of the woman, he enticed her by allowing her a small glimpse of the gold through his spread fingers.

"You see, *señora*, the horses that the *bandido* was leading through your village were stolen from me. They belong to the man I work for, and I have to get them back."

She didn't remove her eyes from his hand, trying to determine the value of the shiny gold that she could barely see between his fingers. "He has not been gone so long, *señor*—thirty minutes perhaps, maybe more. I am not so sure.''

"I have to know more than that, *señora*, before I give up this gold. I saw the tracks of three additional horses leaving in the same direction as the bandit. Did he have friends waiting for him in this village?''

She studied the question at length before answering, wondering if the additional information could perhaps earn her an extra piece of gold, but decided not to risk it. "Those are the tracks of the Americans. They are very bad men, and they follow after the *bandido*, and they will kill him and take the horses which you seek. This is only what I think.''

"How long since the Americans followed after the bandit, *señora*?''

"Oh, not so long ago. Maybe fifteen minutes before you came to this cantina.''

Billy removed his hand from the coin, and the woman snatched it up greedily and deposited it in some mysterious cavity between her breasts, as if expecting him to change his mind.

"Thank you, *señora*,'' Billy said, walking to the door, "you've been a lot of help.''

The country to the south of the village was, for the most part, a vast, desolate wasteland, spotted with tumbleweed and the like, and provided little cover for a rider on horseback. The very thought of approaching either the Mexican or the Americans in such open terrain without a weapon caused Billy some apprehension, but he knew he had no choice but to continue after them, hoping he would not have the need of defending himself along the way.

Daylight was now gone, and as difficult as it would be to keep to the trail in the darkness, it was in his favor. Also, the three Americans who were following the bandit would, undoubtedly, not suspect that they were being trailed as well, and that gave him an element of surprise. He would continue the chase, playing it as he saw it, and hoping for a break when the opportunity for a confrontation with the men presented itself.

Billy had no doubt that he could have found a way to overpower the bandit while he slept, but the unexpected appearance of the Americans now presented him a situation he hadn't bargained for. His only hope, as he could now see it, was to sneak the horses from the camp while the men were either occupied or asleep—assuming, of course, they remained in camp for the night.

Billy could no longer see the tracks in the closing darkness, but he remained on a southerly course, stopping only periodically to verify the existence of the hoofprints he was following by lighting sulphur matches and cupping the flame to conceal his presence.

Less than an hour out of the village, Billy heard a single gunshot, followed seconds later by two more explosions in rapid succession. Then all was quiet. Urging the tired mule with his heels, he sped toward the source of the gunshots, hoping his mount would not trip in the dark and break a leg.

He could now see the light of a distant campfire, and he slowed the mule to a walk and circled the camp at a safe distance.

Dismounting and tying the tired mule to a nearby bush, Billy made his way slowly toward the camp, stooping to keep from presenting a target against the background of the star-filled sky.

From his concealed position in the dark shadows away from the campfire, Billy could now hear the laughter and coarse language of the Americans. Between him and the camp were tied his chestnut and the Mexican's dun horse.

And on the opposite side of the camp, to his disappointment, were the Arabian and the horses of the Americans. Already, Billy concluded, they had cut the Arabian from the other horses in anticipation of taking him with them when they left the camp. That was as he had feared. Instead of spending the night on the range as he had earlier hoped, they gave all the appearances of preparing to head out almost at once.

Weaponless, Billy was at a loss as to his next course of action. If he stayed hidden until the Americans rode off he might be able to trail them to their unknown destination and hope for an opportunity in which to retake the Arabian, or, as a second option, he could create a commotion and hope to spook them into running off and leaving the horse behind.

Either tactic was risky, he figured, but he was short on options, possessing neither a weapon nor the time in which to figure a more masterful plan for taking the Arabian from its captors. So, settling for his latter plan of creating a ruse to spook the Americans, he only hoped that the element of surprise would work in his favor and not come back to haunt him.

Removing the saddles and bridles from the dun horse and the mule, he slapped them on the flanks with his hat and sent them running through the sagebrush at a full gallop. Then, whooping and yelling and creating all the commotion he could for one man, he began circling the camp, hoping to give the outlaws the impression that they were being encircled by a much superior number of men.

"What the—there's somebody out there!" Brogen yelled to the others. "That damn greaser wasn't bluffing after all.

Fisk, take the black horse and run north with him. Me and Beak'll hold them off until you're in the clear.''

"There's one over there!" Beak yelled, firing both six-guns simultaneously at Billy's shadowy figure.

Billy felt a searing pain as a bullet found his left shoulder and he threw himself to the ground. Crawling away quickly on all fours, he sought to relocate to a different position, just in case the outlaws ventured out into the darkness to investigate. Things weren't going at all as he had planned.

"I got one! By doggie I got one!" Beak yelled triumphantly. "I saw him fall."

"Yeah, but I wonder why they're not shooting back." Brogen yelled over the noise of Beak's rapid fire. "Hell, they could be surrounding us! Let's get the hell out of here, partner. Who would have thought that greaser was telling the truth about having *compadres* out here."

"What about the Mex's guns? He had some really nice weapons on him." Beak yelled on the run.

"Well, if you want them, you just go ahead and get them. Me, I'm high-tailing it out of here right now," Brogen said, mounting his horse.

"I don't want them that bad," Beak said, following after him.

Billy lay where he had hidden himself beneath a low-growing bush until he heard the hoofbeats subside. Then, holding his hand over his wound, he made his way cautiously into the Mexican's camp.

He found the bandit lying dead with his six-gun near his outstretched hand and a plate of beans scattered about his feet. Apparently, the outlaws had bushwhacked the Mexican while he was eating, shooting him before he could defend himself. He had taken two bullets in his back, another in his head.

Throwing more sticks on the dying fire, Billy ripped off the bloody sleeve from his brand-new shirt and checked the wound. It was only a graze, and he had naturally figured it to be much worse because of the resultant blood and pain. Ripping off the remaining sleeve, he used water from his canteen to cleanse the wound. Making an impromptu bandage using the clean sleeve from his shirt, he began a search of the Mexican's camp, seeking his stolen property.

Going through the bandit's belongings, he finally rounded up his six-gun and rifle and checked them for loads. Rolling the dead man over, he retrieved his pouch of gold and started for the chestnut.

He was happy having the familiar chestnut once again underneath him. The mule had been a good mount for a mule, he had to admit, but the long-legged chestnut gelding was a far better one for speed.

Retracing his earlier trail in the moonlight, he paced the chestnut to keep from tiring him too quickly. His horse, although riderless, had been on the trail since early light, and he had no idea of the condition of the outlaws' horses, or how far they would ride before stopping to rest them, and he had to be prepared for the worst situation by conserving his own mount as much as possible.

All indications told Billy that the outlaws were heading back to the little village where they had taken up the bandit's trail. It was very doubtful, he figured, that they would risk spending the night in the village, but he certainly hoped they would. He'd had enough for one day.

Riding at a leisurely pace, Billy was reminded of his intense hunger, and wished that he had taken the time to eat back at the Mexican's camp. He hadn't eaten since the night before, and he was now beginning to weaken from hunger, as well as from his weariness at being in the saddle for two days.

Even if the three outlaws didn't put up for the night in the village, he decided that he would try to round up some grub without having to lose valuable time by cooking it himself. For if he found himself having to track the outlaws over a long distance, he didn't want to risk getting so far behind them that a sudden rainstorm might come along to obliterate their tracks.

Soon, he could see several flickering lights in the distance that indicated the village. Tense with the uncertainty of the sort of welcome he might expect at the cantina, should the outlaws be there, he removed the six-gun from its holster and again checked the loads.

Veering off the well-traveled trail, Billy approached the cantina from the back side as he had done previously. If the outlaws had decided to spend the night in the village, it was probable that they would put up the horses in the village's only corral.

But except for a couple of burros and mules, the corral was empty. Dismounting, he led the chestnut around the building to an empty hitching rail and tied him off.

Inside the cantina were several young Mexicans drinking in a far corner, and they stared at him curiously as he approached the woman behind the bar.

"You again, so soon. Did you not find the horses you were seeking?"

"Yes and no," Billy told the woman. "The three Americans beat me to the black horse I was after. Did you see them ride through here earlier?"

"See them, no, but I heard the sound of several horses riding in from the south, heading north through the village not so long ago. But they rode through without stopping here. Perhaps they were the men you speak of?''

"Most likely so," Billy said thoughtfully.

"*Señor*, you appear so very tired. Perhaps you would like something to drink—*pulque* . . . water?''

"No, thank you, but I am powerful hungry. Do you have anything to eat in this place?''

"Oh, *si*, but it is beans and *tortillas* only.''

"Beans and *tortillas* would do me just fine, *señora*. I'll have something now, and you can fix me something for the trail, if that's possible.''

Billy was ravenous, and ate the second serving offered him by the bemused woman behind the bar. While he ate, she made him a package consisting of the same fare, wrapped in corn shucks.

Removing the gold pouch, he handed the wide-eyed woman a small gold piece and resumed his meal. He failed to notice the looks exchanged by the three Mexicans who were watching him from the back of the cantina.

As Billy was putting away the last of the simple fare placed in front of him, the three young Mexicans who had been studying him all the while, spoke to the woman in Spanish and walked quietly into the night. Alone, the woman smiled at him, brushing back her hair with her hand as she leaned across the bar provocatively and said, "Such a young man as yourself should have a warm bed on a night like this, *señor*. I, Maria, have such a bed. I am not so young as before, but I am experienced in providing the needs of a young man like yourself. Believe me when I say this.''

"Uh . . . thanks just the same, *señora*. I'm certain what you say is true, and the loss is probably mine, but I have to be getting along.''

Taking his food, Billy left the reflective woman leaning on the bar and walked outside.

Before Billy could take the reins from the hitching rail, two clenched fists came down hard on his shoulders, knocking him to his knees, and almost instantly two more shadowy figures emerged and joined the bigger Mexican who had sucker-punched him.

Not taking the time to figure it out, Billy's reaction was instantaneous. Rolling beneath the hitching rail to put it between his attackers and himself, he jumped quickly to his feet and grabbed the neck of the man who had hit him, and, with all the strength he could muster from his two hundred pounds, dropped to the ground, bringing the man's face down against the cross rail with a bone-shattering force that rendered him unconscious.

Billy failed to get a purchase on the next man, who wrenched free from his grasp and fled after the third man who had already vanished into the safety of the night.

Stepping over the prostrate man whom he had laid out with the hitching rail, Billy rubbed his aching shoulders and mounted the chestnut. The food he had intended to carry with him on the trail lay scattered in the dust where he had dropped it.

He knew he was in no condition to chase after the outlaws, what with his lack of rest from his day's ride, and the burning sensation to his left shoulder where he had earlier taken the bullet, not to mention the aching from the punch he had taken moments ago in front of the cantina. Besides, he didn't want to risk losing the outlaws' trail in the dark and finding himself having to backtrack.

All that considered, Billy rode a safe distance from the village and reined into a cottonwood thicket along the Pecos and made a dry camp. He still considered himself yet close enough to the village to be endangered, should any of the three men who had earlier attempted to rob him come in on him while he slept. But he thought they wouldn't try that again, particularly after their first attempt didn't exactly go the way they had obviously planned it.

Chances were, Billy figured, the outlaws themselves would have to camp sometime during the night. He certainly hoped so. It would cut the distance that separated them if they had to pull off the trail and grab some sleep themselves.

Chapter 7

In the fleeting darkness of the approaching new day, Billy watered the chestnut in the Pecos, then made his way back to the trail. He was weak from hunger, and although he still had a bit of flour and bacon in his warbag he didn't wish to take the time to cook it. He cursed the three Mexicans who had jumped him outside the cantina and caused him to lose the food that was meant for the trail.

Later, Billy rode upon the outlaws' camp of the night before, and the ashes of their fire was still warm, telling him that he wasn't all that far behind them. He could also discern the signs of their having cooked and eaten before riding out.

All was as he had earlier hoped: their stopping to sleep and cook breakfast had served to cut the distance that separated them, and he estimated that he was no more than a couple of hours behind the outlaws. If he pressed the chestnut without overheating him, he could expect to shorten the distance between them even more.

After a couple of hours of steady riding, Billy followed the outlaws' tracks into foothills that were desolate and rocky, and, for the most part, devoid of living vegetation. All about him, cliffs of exposed strata that had shifted and cracked with eons of time only added to the strangeness of the unfamiliar terrain in which he now found himself.

For a while longer, periodically stopping to give his horse

a breather, Billy followed the outlaws' tracks through the wasteland, all the while reaching elevations that afforded him a panoramic view of the plains below.

For hours, it seemed, the landscape was unchanged, and it was with relief Billy abruptly found himself in a small green valley, with aspens and cottonwoods bordering a running stream. From either side of the valley floor, where carpets of lush grass grew as high as the chestnut's fetlocks, rose sheer, peaked cliffs of solid rock.

Just inside a wide defile that was the entrance to the valley, Billy drew up the gelding and studied the precipitous walls which encircled him. From what he could see of his surroundings, the place was completely bottled in, and there appeared no other exit for the outlaws except by way of the opening he had entered.

If this was where the desperados maintained their permanent base, they had themselves a good hideout, Billy thought; even if a pursuing posse discovered the entrance, they would likely be unable to storm their way through the opening if it were properly defended, and if need be, the outlaws could hole up for as long as their food and ammo held out.

Either owing to their lack of manpower, or else not believing that they would be followed into the valley, the outlaws had not posted a guard at the entrance, which was fortunate for Billy, as he had ridden into it completely unaware that he had found their hideout.

He was tired now—awfully tired—and his shoulders were still sore from the blow he had taken from the man in front of the cantina. His bullet wound was raw and stinging, and he was hungry.

The chestnut needed a rubdown and a good rest, so the immediate thing to do was find an isolated spot among the trees and rest until dark, when there was less risk of being spotted by the outlaws when he approached them.

Somewhere in the beautiful valley was the Arabian, of this he had no doubt, and when he found the outlaws he would also find the horse. But whatever lay ahead for him, he would need rest in order to regain his strength. In the thickest part of the cottonwoods he unsaddled his horse and rubbed him down with dry grass and leaves, then he watered him in the stream and fed him on grass that grew abundantly along the bank.

After attending to the needs of the chestnut, Billy removed the bloody bandage from his shoulder and cleaned his wound with water from the stream. Feeling somewhat better now, with the chores out of his way, he rested against a tree and cut small strips of lean from his remaining bacon and consumed it uncooked. As badly as he needed nourishment he didn't want to risk a fire that would give away his presence.

Billy had only intended to sleep for a short while so that he would be alert for the job that lay ahead of him, but it was after dark when he was awakened by the smell of smoke and cooking food. Jumping quickly to his feet, he saddled the chestnut and gathered his gear and made ready for a quick getaway, should it become necessary.

The pleasant aroma of roasting meat hung heavy in the air, causing his stomach to growl, and he knew the outlaws had to be very near his position. Checking his six-gun, he left loose the leather thong that secured it in its holster, then began to make his way through the darkened forest, using random shafts of penetrating moonlight to find his way to the source of the muffled voices.

As he neared their camp, the voices of the outlaws became clearer, and Billy could overhear them discussing the ransom that the Arabian might bring them when they made

their demands of its owner, and presently he could see the
light of their fire through the thick growth from where he
stood concealed.

The open meadow where the outlaws made their camp
was awash in the light of a full moon, and Billy began to
take in his surroundings. Behind where the outlaws sat relaxed around their campfire was an old, roofless cabin built
of mud-chinked rocks and logs, and approximately fifty feet
beyond them in the opposite direction was a corral containing their horses. And although Billy couldn't make out
the Arabian for certain at that distance, there was little doubt
in his mind that he was there with the other horses.

Even from the distance where he lay hidden, Billy began
to see in the three men who sat around the campfire something familiar, and after close scrutiny he was surprised to
recognize them as the men who had shared the dining room
with him in Las Cumbres, several days previously.

From his concealment in the shadow of the trees, he began
to make plans for surprising and disarming the outlaws
without causing bloodshed. He was not a violent person by
nature, and it was only in his own self-defense that he had
ever resorted to inflicting hurt on another person. So, to
remove the Arabian from the camp of the outlaws without
either them or himself getting hurt or killed meant careful
planning.

The men were out of six-gun range from where he stood,
and too much open ground lay between them to effect a
surprise, so Billy hadn't much choice but to circle behind
the cabin and place himself closer to his target. That meant
leaving the concealment of the trees and putting himself in
the open for a short distance, but he figured that by staying
in the shadows he would be able to pull it off.

Perhaps there were others about, too, but he somehow

doubted that. The very fact that the outlaws had not posted a lookout at the entrance to the valley told him they had not been expected to be followed to their hideout. Most likely, Billy surmised, the outlaws attached no importance to their security when they thought that they were only dealing with a gang of *bandidos* back on the trail.

As he began to backtrack in order to circle behind the cabin, Billy was making tentative plans to step from the shadows of the far side of the structure closest to the outlaws and surprise them at point-blank range. Once he managed to disarm them he would take their mounts and scatter them to keep from being overtaken on the trail to Bent Rock. By the time they managed to round up their horses, he should be too far along for them to even consider chasing after him.

Reaching a point where the trees gave way to a vast open area, Billy was forced to make his way cautiously along the base of the sheer cliff that towered above the cabin opposite where the outlaws sat around their campfire. Having the shadow of the solid-rock projection as his only source of concealment, he had to be careful in his movements. Any small noise he made that would attract their attention could leave him in the open without any defense from their bullets.

Taking one agonizing step at the time, Billy slowly picked his way along the base of the cliff. With his six-gun in his hand, he kept a watchful eye on the outlaws. Never in his entire life had he felt so vulnerable, and he figured his chances of coming out on top against three guns were slim to none.

It was as he was about to make his big move to put the cabin between himself and the outlaws that it happened. Billy inadvertently dislodged a large rock that went cascading several feet down the slope. Freezing where he stood, he trained his gun on the startled men.

"Listen! You jaspers hear that?" Brogen asked, pulling his gun.

"Just a rock falling down the slope. Happens all the time," Beak replied.

"I reckon so," Brogen agreed reluctantly.

Billy remained frozen in his position until the outlaws lost interest in the noise and resumed their interrupted conversation. Had they not been staring into the fire, he figured, they might have noticed the light-colored shirt he wore.

Quickly now, before the outlaws decided to turn in for the night and make his confrontation with them more difficult, Billy made his way to the safety of the cabin wall. Creeping softly to the opposite corner, where the shadow of the cabin met the reflected light of the fire, he drew up and prepared himself for what he was about to do.

Never in his entire life had he pointed a gun at any man, and to do so now took all the courage he could muster. For to draw on a man meant there existed the possibility of bloodshed—either his or theirs—and that was exactly the thing he meant to avoid, if at all possible.

Taking a deep breath to calm his racing heart, Billy stepped from the shadow of the cabin with his six-gun extended and said, "Stand up and remove your gun belts, gents. Do it now!"

The outlaws did not appear too rattled by the kid's appearance, nor by his demand, but rather looked at him in amusement without reacting to his order to relinquish their guns. This Billy had not expected, but he managed to maintain his composure and hold his ground.

"Well, just you looky here," Beak said derisively. "Boy, didn't your pa ever tell you not to point that thing at a grown man? Now put it away before I take it from you and spank you with it.''

"Hey, ain't I seen you somewheres?'' Brogen said, lifting his thick eyebrows. "Yeah, now I remember, it was a few days ago in Las Cumbres. Ain't you a mite young for a bounty hunter, kid?''

"Enough palavering,'' Billy said, his confidence now growing. "Just drop those gun belts like I done told you.''

"And just what are you going to do about it if we don't?'' Beak jeered. "You think you can take us all before one of us plugs you?''

"I guess I'll just take you first—if it comes to that. Now for the last time, drop your guns.'' To punctuate his demand, Billy fired a round between Beak's feet, causing the little man to jump into the air in surprise.

Slowly, Beak pretended to unbuckle his belt, then, with lightning speed, his right hand went for his six-gun, but the gun barely cleared the holster before Billy's .44 belched flame, sending the slight man flying backwards. It was a clean hit to the heart, and the once-notorious desperado, who had a dozen notches on his guns, never felt the impact of the bullet that ended his long career.

Brogen, whose shooting hand was part-way to his gun when the explosion filled the night, froze in fear and obedience. Finding his voice at last, he said, "Just who the hell are you, kid? Why are you hassling us, anyhow?''

"I belong to that black stallion you jaspers took from the Mexican. Actually, it belongs to my boss, but I'm the one responsible for it.''

"Now just you hold on there, mister. You trying to accuse us of stealing that horse? Why, my partners and me saved it from that Mex what stole it. We figured to see it back to its rightful owner, sure enough. For a fancy horse like that black, figured there might be a nice reward for recovering it.''

''That why you shot the Mexican in the back while he was eating?''

''That bean-eating thief was a-fixing to take that horse to Mexico. We did you a big favor by plugging him, and how do you repay us? Why, you shoot down our little partner, that's how.''

''That's right, mister,'' Fisk said mournfully, ''you've gunned down an innocent man.''

''Yeah,'' Brogen joined in, ''you best take your blamed horse and leave us to bury our little partner.''

''I have every intention of leaving with the horse—with or without your permission—but I don't aim to be bush-whacked in the process. Now remove your gun belts and drop them where you stand. But you best be slow about it. My six-gun has a hair-trigger.''

Billy caught the signal between the two outlaws, imperceptible though it was, and to impress them with the seriousness of his intent, he pulled back the hammer and pointed it at Brogen. ''I said easy does it, partners.''

At this, the men immediately dropped their gun belts at their feet and glared at Billy. ''Now, gents, step back to the other side of the fire and add some wood, but be nice and slow about it. I'm here to tell you, I'm in no mood for funny stuff.''

After the fire was blazing, Billy emptied the bullets from the six-guns and tossed them unceremoniously into the blaze, catching the startled expressions on the outlaws' faces. ''Where are your rifles?'' he asked Brogen.

''Over yonder,'' Brogen growled, pointing to the three rifles leaning against the cabin wall, a few feet away. ''Ah, come on, kid, you ain't gonna destroy my rifle, are you? That's a custom gun.''

"Yeah, and you most likely stole it," Billy replied non-chalantly, giving the rifles the same send-off as the six-guns.

"Now," Billy said, waving his gun at the outlaws, "walk in front of me to the corral, and no tricks."

Openly fuming, Brogen took the lead to where the horses were corraled, and Billy could see the anger welling up in him. Having been the one to give orders for most of his life, he was not accustomed to taking them from anyone, and the realization that he was being bullied by a mere kid was almost too much for his oversized ego.

"You," Billy said to Fisk, once they reached the corral, "saddle one of the horses." And to Brogen he said, "You will string the remainder of the horses to the saddle horn, and I want the black stallion in the lead."

"Now just a darn minute, kid," Brogen said heatedly. "You don't mean to say you're really taking our horses and leaving us stranded on this mountain, miles from civilization. I mean, it's bad enough you destroyed our guns."

"Oh, stop your bellyaching, you owlhoot. I'll turn your horses loose down the trail a-ways. You can round them up come daylight—after I'm long gone from these parts."

The horses were soon ready to travel as Billy had demanded, but before mounting, he rechecked the cinch. He didn't trust anyone to saddle the horse he was about to ride, particularly an outlaw. Satisfied, he then made certain that the Arabian's lead rope was secured before climbing into the saddle.

Waving his six-gun toward the nearby cliffs, Billy said, "You gents see that lone coyote outlined against the moon up there? Well, go up there and tell him howdy."

"Walk clear up there—at night? You got to be loco, kid. I just ain't gonna do it," Brogen said adamantly. "A body could get hurt climbing up there in the dark."

"Either that or get shot. I leave the choice to you."

The outlaws reluctantly walked out a distance and stopped and looked back at Billy defiantly. He fired a couple of rounds just over their heads that sent them scurrying up the incline.

Quickly, Billy made tracks for the far side of the cotton-wood grove, where the chestnut was saddled and waiting.

Once in his familiar saddle, Billy found the trail in the moonlight and led the string of horses through the defile and out of the valley. It would be slow going for a few miles yet, he knew; the ground was littered with rocks and boulders and washes, making night riding hazardous for both man and animal.

Particularly, Billy was concerned about the Arabian. He dreaded the thought that he'd gone through the last several days chasing after the horse, only to expose him to the possibility of a broken leg.

In spite of his hunger and his wound, his lack of proper rest and his overall weariness, Billy felt shut of the tension which had plagued him since the very first moment when the Arabian bolted free at the train station. Never in all his born days could he recall an animal which had caused him so much trouble and misery. And so happy was he to have the horse back in his custody that it had slipped his mind entirely that his original motive for capturing him was to make a favorable impression on Sanderson's beautiful daughter.

Billy found it hard going on the mountain trail, even traveling by the light of a full moon. The chestnut, which was the best all-around horse he had ever ridden, chose his footing on the rocky inclines with a caution born of experience.

He judged it had been more than an hour since he exited the valley, a safe enough distance to release the outlaws' horses. Dallying the Arabian's lead rope around his saddle horn, Billy scattered the remaining string and continued on into the night.

He disliked leaving anyone stranded without horses and guns, particularly in the wilds of the mountain country, but by their very actions they had brought it on themselves. At least they had their lives, which was more than could be said for their partner—and the Mexican they had dispatched earlier.

The outlaws were men habitually accustomed to the hardships of this country, Billy knew, and he felt they had come out of the encounter in fair shape. Some men in a similar situation would have shot them on sight as horse thieves— or else hung them from a tree for all to see. Oh, they would be cussing up a blue steak while they chased their horses through the hills, but that only served them right.

The short nap Billy had taken earlier under the cottonwoods had done him a world of good, but still he was tired and needed sleep, and he had visions of the bed back at the Tivoli. This time, he felt, he could even sleep on the soft down mattress without a problem. He had paid a week's advance rent on the room and had used it only one night.

And it was likely the expensive room might continue to go unused; he hadn't made up his mind about that one yet. With the trouble he'd had because of the Arabian, he was seriously contemplating throwing his bedroll on the stable floor to provide security for the elusive horse.

Several times throughout the long night, Billy stopped to allow the horses to rest and drink from a stream. He was tempted, each time he stopped, to lean against a rock and catch a nap, if only for a few minutes, but he knew that once he closed his eyes he wouldn't open them again for hours.

More than a few times, Billy caught himself dozing in the saddle, jerking awake when there was an appreciable change in the chestnut's motion. Once, he dismounted and led the horse in a vain attempt at walking off his sleepiness, but it accomplished nothing, and served only to cost him valuable time.

It was with a great relief that Billy finally rode upon the little adobe huts that marked the outskirts of Bent Rock. Even the barking dogs that ran out into the street to harass the horses sent a thrill through him; it meant civilization, food, a hot bath, and, most blessed of all, sleep.

For the most part, the town was not yet awake, and all about him roosters crowed and strutted their virility, while poor Mexican laborers were beginning to hit the streets, shuffling about in their early-morning catalepsy. From across town came the sounds of a steam engine switching cattle cars near the shipping pens.

At the livery stable, Billy arranged for a stall to house the Arabian, flipping the stableboy a gold coin to provide the horse special attention and security. After he was assured the proper care of both the Arabian and the chestnut, he dragged himself wearily to the hotel, determined to sleep for at least the next two days.

Sitting on the edge of the bed, Billy removed a boot, then lay back to rest a moment before removing the other, and that was the last he remembered—until Effie Sanderson's shrill voice intruded on his dreams.

Chapter 8

"Mr. Bayes, please wake up," came the shrill voice of Effie Sanderson through Billy's sleep fog. "Please, you *must* wake up."

"Go way, ma'am," he whispered tiredly. "I need sleep. Whatever it is, I don't care . . . just leave me be, for crying out loud."

"Sleepy or not, young man, you simply must get out of bed." Eyeing the pitcher of water on the bedside commode, she grabbed it and poured its contents in Billy's face.

"Thunderations! What was that for?" Billy bellowed, flailing his arms and jerking himself into a sitting position.

"It was to get your attention, and apparently it worked. My niece is gone and you have to go after her right away."

"What do you mean, gone? What are you saying, ma'am?" Disoriented by his lack of sleep, the woman's words made no sense to Billy whatsoever.

"How much clearer can I state it, young man? I have a note from her saying she intended to ride into those hills and look for you and that horse."

"So what do you want me to do about it, ma'am? She's a big girl."

"What do I want you to do about it, indeed! Why, I want you to go and find her and bring her safely back to town. She was terribly worried when you had not returned with the Arabian last night. She feels responsible for that horse and thinks she let her father down. She has always been too headstrong for her own good.''

''I wouldn't worry too much, ma'am. She strikes me as a girl who can look out for herself.''

''It does not concern you, young man, that she is running around in that wilderness in search of you and that horse? Why, most anything could happen to a young, defenseless girl out there alone. You must go after her at once. I am not making a request; I am giving you an order to go after my niece and bring her back at once.''

''Please don't say that, ma'am. I've been out there for three days and nights. I've been robbed and shot; I haven't eaten or got any sleep to amount to much, and I had to kill a man—my first. On top of it all, I still feel like I'm sitting in the saddle. Can't it wait?''

''No! Absolutely not. Now put your other boot on and go after her this very minute. That child could be in serious trouble.''

''Oh, ma'am, you just don't understand. I don't think I could mount a horse right now. Besides, my horse is worn out. He isn't up to another trip without a rest.''

''Then rent one from the livery. According to her note that is what my niece did.''

''Ma'am, I wouldn't know where to start looking for her. It's a mighty big country out there, you know.''

''Big country—pshaw! All this country is the same. Just pick up her trail where the Arabian bolted the other morning. Her tracks will be fresh . . . even I know that much.''

''I'll do what I can, ma'am, but I can't guarantee anything.''

''That is as much as I can ask, Mr. Bayes. And by the way, did you find the Arabian?''

"Yes, ma'am, I did. He's at the livery behind the hotel. He's all right."

"Well, that is most certainly a consolation, at least. You can fill me in on the details of it later. And young man . . ."

"Ma'am?"

"You *will* find my niece and escort her safely back to town."

The sidewalks and streets were crowded with people walking about, and they gave Billy a wide berth as he staggered from the hotel and made his way to the livery, still wearing the same clothing of the last several days.

The fact that his shirt was dirty and bloodied and missing both sleeves, and that he had neither taken a bath nor shaved in several days, was the very least of his worries. That he was in a poor condition to mount a horse was also apparent to him, but his strong sense of loyalty to his employer would give him the needed strength to do what he knew was expected of him.

It was true that the girl was taking a risk by riding out alone in the surrounding hills, what with mountain lions around that had been known to attack men and horses. And there were bandits about, an indisputable fact for which he could personally vouch.

From the kid at the livery stable, Billy learned that the girl had rented a horse and ridden out just moments before he had arrived back in town, and had he not ridden in by a different route he might have met her and saved himself the extra trouble he was now being put to by her concerned aunt. But that was neither here nor there, he concluded.

Billy rented a piebald mare that was a little too skittish for his liking, but it was the last rental horse the livery had for any amount of money, and it had to do the job in order that his chestnut get some much needed rest. After having chased all over the country for the past several days, he knew that the chestnut had been pushed to the limit, as had he himself.

Saddled and outfitted, Billy rode down past the train depot and out into the foothills. Taking to the tracks of several days previous, he had no difficulty in picking up a fresh set of tracks over the original ones made by the Arabian and the chestnut. This time, he decided, he would simply eliminate many of the detours made by the Arabian and head straight for his old campsite.

By eliminating such detours, he could cut much time from the ride and, perhaps, even beat the girl to the camp. He only hoped that she encountered no problems which would prevent her from showing up at the point where he hoped to meet up with her. In that event, he would have to backtrack until he found her.

Billy determined that the girl was pushing it too hard early on, and if she continued at that reckless pace she would soon lather her mount, risking even more problems. He wondered whether she had enough horse savvy to recognize their limits. Surely, he thought, she would have learned something about horses in those nine years she had spent on the Rocking J, before going East to live with her aunt.

And just as Billy had hoped, the cut of the tracks indicated to him that she had slowed her horse to a walk. It was out of her excitement to be on the trail, perhaps, that she had begun her search at such a fast clip.

By picking out landmarks he recognized from his first trip into the foothills, Billy was making good time, and had no difficulty in keeping to a straight course. The girl, he figured, was running around in circles, as he had done when he followed the Arabian's meandering tracks earlier.

At his destination, Billy was at once aware of the odor of death. He had completely forgotten about the dead Mexican. The piebald balked at entering the trees where the odor was strongest, and he had to tie her to a nearby cedar and go in on foot.

There at his old campsite remained only the scattered bones of the bandit, picked clean by vultures and small animals. Considering the nauseating smell of death, Billy was relieved to find he had beaten the girl to the site.

Knowing that he would have to wait for the girl to show up there, Billy decided to do the Christian thing and cover the bones of the bandit while he waited. It really wasn't that much of a chore, except for having to round up the scattered bones—and the odor. Sooner than he expected he had enough rocks with which to cover the condensed remains, and he cut a crude cross from a tree limb with his hunting knife and tied the sticks together with a strip of leather he carried in his warbag.

Finished, the girl still had not shown, and Billy was now concerned. She had not more than a hour's start on him, and, even by taking her time, she should have ridden up to the camp long before now. The fact that she was this late did not bode well with him, and he began to sense that something unexplained had befallen her on the trail.

Kicking himself for not following her tracks from the offset, he started down the trail that the Arabian and the chestnut had made several days back. Somewhere along that meandering route taken by the Arabian should be the tracks of her horse—or at least the signs where she either lost the trail or purposely turned off it. Whichever was the case, he would figure it out.

His thoughts kept running to the girl. Was she out looking for him or the horse? He wondered. After thinking on it, he had to conclude that it was really the horse that had her worried. After all, she had a responsibility to the horse, and she didn't even know him. He was embarrassed that he had allowed his ego to become so over-inflated.

Billy was having difficulty in keeping his eyes open, and several times he dozed in the saddle and found himself off the trail and had to circle to put himself back on the tracks. Coming to a pool of standing water in an arroyo, he watered the piebald and wet his face to keep awake.

Hungry, he remembered the newspaper-wrapped package of food that Effie Sanderson had prepared for him in the hotel dining room. It consisted mostly of chunks of beef and thick slices of bread, which he wolfed down before it occurred to him that he should have saved part of it for the girl, in case they met some delay in getting back to town.

Billy did not remember closing his eyes at all, and when he was startled awake by the sounds of the piebald blowing, he was surprised to see that the sun was precariously close to sinking over the distant mountains.

In a panic, he climbed into the saddle and made his way back to the point where he had earlier left the trail in order to water the horse. There, Billy saw the tracks he recognized to be those of the horse the girl was riding, and she was heading in the direction from which he had earlier ridden before leaving the trail. He had inadvertently fallen asleep and missed her. "Darn!" he swore aloud, startling the horse. "Another screwup."

Well, all was not really lost, he figured. If he hurried the piebald he might just catch up to her before dark, but he couldn't see any way out of having to spend the night under the stars. The big bed back at the Tivoli Hotel was becoming an elusive dream.

Now strengthened by the food he had earlier eaten, and

decidedly more alert as a result of the several hours of sleep he had gotten, Billy could feel his old energy returning. Putting the spurs to the equally rested piebald, he followed the trail at a gallop. It was the fast approaching darkness that now had him worried.

Taking his eyes off the tracks only long enough to look over his shoulder at the sun's position, Billy was momentarily confused when he returned his attention to the trail and the hoof marks were no longer there. Reining in quickly, he let fly a string of dark expletives and started backtracking.

Approximately fifty feet up the trail Billy stopped his horse and studied the confusing signs in front of him. The shod tracks of two additional horses joined those of the girl's mount, and together all three headed north across the ridge back.

Studying the new tracks, Billy felt a cold, tingling sensation traverse the entire length of his spine. He recognized the new hoofprints; he had trailed them the entire day before. They belonged to the horses of the outlaws who called themselves Brogen and Fisk. How they had managed to collect their horses and make it to the area so quickly left him puzzled.

This was about the worst thing that could possibly happen, as Billy saw it. The outlaws, who had undoubtedly taken the girl against her wishes, were not the type of men who would honor the unwritten code of female sanctity. His adrenalin flowing, he pushed the piebald to her limit, and when he felt that the horse was holding back on him, he raked her shoulders with his rowels, getting a new burst of speed in response. He must not lose the trail in the fast approaching darkness; to wait for daylight might be too late to save the girl's honor at the hands of her captors—if not her life.

Clearing a rise in the dying light, Billy saw the three hobbled horses that were grazing peacefully in a clearing near the tree line. He pulled the piebald to an abrupt stop, then just as quickly swung her in the direction from which he came. He only hoped his reaction was quick enough to prevent the outlaws from spotting him.

Tethering the piebald to a scraggly bush, Billy began to circle the ridge in hopes of catching the outlaws by surprise. It was almost dark enough now to provide him the necessary cover in which to sneak in on them unobserved, and his only worry was that he might have been seen when he exposed himself momentarily on the rise.

Quickly finding himself in the cottonwood grove, Billy began to step quietly from tree to tree, using them as a cover while he made his way toward where he figured the outlaws had set up their camp for the night. He could hear no sounds of talking, and that bothered him. With three people around, there should be at least some audible signs of their presence. Unless . . . they were expecting him.

Moving now with more caution than ever, Billy stood longer at each position behind the tree trunks, becoming increasingly confused as to why he neither saw nor heard the outlaws.

Then Billy heard a snapping sound that he knew to be a dry twig being stepped on. Cold beads of perspiration broke out on his forehead, and he slowly let his hand fall to his six-gun. But he never made it, feeling the solid impact to the back of his head, pain followed by a white flash, then total darkness.

Groggy and in pain, Billy opened his eyes and oriented himself. It took several minutes for him to realize where he was and what had happened to him. He tried to feel his head wound and found that his hands were bound behind him to a cottonwood sapling and that he was facing a camp-fire which was a good twenty feet away from his position

The outlaws, Brogen and Fisk, were squatting next to the fire with their backs to Billy, and neither seemed aware that he was now conscious and watching them.

Facing his left, only a few feet away, the girl was also sitting against a sapling, her hands behind her. "Psst, Miss Sanderson, are you all right? Have they hurt you?" Billy whispered.

"Oh, you're awake now," she whispered back. "I was so worried that they'd hit you too hard. There was so much blood when they dragged you here and tied you."

"But what about you, ma'am? Did they hurt you?"

"Not yet they haven't, but I'm terribly frightened of the one called Fisk. He seems too interested in me."

"Try and hold yourself together, miss. No matter what happens, don't fall apart on me."

"I'll certainly try, Mr. Bayes, but I'm so frightened of those men. I heard them discussing having their way with me, and there isn't a thing I can do about it."

"Hey, just what is all that whispering about over there?" Brogen yelled. "There'll be no talking, you two." Both outlaws came and stood looking down at Billy.

"Well, well, just you looky here, Fisk. I didn't kill the pole cat after all. Must be losing my touch in my old age."

"There's no doubt about it, partner, but look on the bright side. A sneaky sidewinder like him deserves to die a real slow death. You see, there's a few tricks I picked up from the Apaches that should be interesting to try out on him. What do you think about that?" Fisk grinned through his beard and spat a stream of Burley between Billy's out-stretched legs.

Brogen placed his hands on his hips and stared down at

Billy speculatively and said, "Kid, I shore am glad to see you. Feared there for a spell I'd never get my chance to thank you for gunning down my little partner, not to mention you making a fool out of us like you did up there. Oh, this is going to be so good. You're going to die an inch at a time for what you caused us."

"Maybe he'd like to watch while we have our fun with the little lady," Fisk said, rubbing the girl's hair.

"Well, if you really think he can stand it, partner. I seen what you call having fun with the ladies, and even I can't take it."

"Oh, but I expect she's going to enjoy it," Fisk said, now caressing her face with the back of his hand. "Yes, a beautiful girl like her . . . real gentry, you ask me. And I'll wager she's never had a man—not a real man at least. That's my favorite kind."

"Leave her alone, you low-life varmints. You lay a hand on her and this country won't be big enough to hide you. Her father will see you hunted down like ordinary animals. And believe me, I know her father well."

"And just who might her father be?" Brogen sneered.

"Paul Sanderson, of the Rocking J spread."

"Sanderson!" Brogen hooted. "Why, we're plumb shaking in our boots, kid. Hell fire, we been stealing his cattle and horses for years, and he ain't laid a hand on us."

"You do harm to his daughter, and you'll see different," Billy said calmly.

Snarling, Brogen pretended to walk off, then turned sharply and laid the toes of his boots in Billy's ribcage, causing the girl to scream out hysterically. "Don't hurt him—please! Do what you will with me, but don't hurt him."

"Now that sounds like a pretty good deal to me," Brogen laughed.

"Can you beat that?" Fisk said to the grimacing Billy. "This pretty little thing has up and offered herself to save you a beating. I sure hope you're grateful for that. See, we have plans to use her anyway, and her being willing just makes it all the more fun."

"You lay a hand on her and I'll personally shoot you down, and that's a promise," Billy said heatedly.

"Why, you ain't in a position to threaten nobody this time, kid. Besides, your days are numbered," Brogen laughed.

"I'm going to finish my grub," Fisk said. "Then I'll be back for my dessert. Just you get rid of that sour puss and start thinking sweet thoughts, little missy. We'll have our fun directly."

While Fisk resumed his eating, Brogen squatted beside Billy and continued to taunt him. "I guess you thought you was pretty damn slick back at my hideout, destroying our guns like you did." Brogen removed his six-gun and waved it in Billy's face menacingly.

"Only a idjit would fail to look inside that old cabin. Why, we got us a whole damn arsenal cached there. And them horses, they was back in the corral by first light. You see, they knowed it was the only place on that mountain where they could find grass and water. Them horses, they got more sense than you."

"Look, Brogen," Billy said quietly, "why don't you just turn the girl loose and send her back to town. It's me you got a beef with, not her. Just put her on a horse and let her go."

"I couldn't do that, kid, even if I was of a mind to. My

partner needs her, and when he gets that need, can't nobody stop him.''

Brogen lowered his voice to a near-whisper and said, ''Truth is, I want her myself. She's just about the purtiest little thing I ever laid eyes on, and I ain't ever had a woman looks that good.''

While the outlaws talked, Billy was busy with his ropes. When Brogen had kicked him moments earlier, he had re-coiled in an attempt to shield his body, and the strain against his binds caused his right hand to slip free. Now, using that free hand, he quickly picked at the knot that bound the remaining wrist. In a matter of minutes he would be free, of this he was certain, and already he was assessing the rocks at his feet, looking for one to use as a weapon.

The girl, who had a good view of Billy's busy fingers, picked up on his plan and created a diversion in order to allow him the needed time in which to follow through with his escape attempt. ''Mr. Brogen,'' she said, forcing a se-ductive attitude, ''I really don't care for Mr. Fisk, if you want the truth of the matter, but for a mature man like yourself, I would be willing to do anything—anything at all.''

''Yeah? You like older men, do you?'' Brogen said sheepishly, walking over to her and squatting with his back to Billy.

''Yes, I do. Don't ask me to explain it, but there is something about mature men that seems to bring out the woman in me.''

While Brogen was falling for one of the oldest lines since the origin of the species, Billy was busy grasping a large rock between his feet and bringing it within the reach of his hands by pulling his knees against his chest. Quickly taking the rock and placing it behind him he re-straightened his legs. He was now prepared to react at a moment's notice, and had only to wait for the girl to do her part and further distract the outlaw.

Having seen Billy take the rock, the girl went into action. "Mr. Brogen, would you think it forward of me if I asked to kiss your cheek? I've been dying to do so ever since I first saw you."

"Why heck no, missy. I would plumb consider it an honor. But please," he said in a near whisper, "the name's Elroy."

Closing his eyes and bending down to place his cheek in the girl's face, he was unaware of Billy until the rock that came crashing against his right temple.

Fisk, who caught the action from where he sat eating, reached for his gun, but Billy was already spouting flame with Brogen's commandeered six-gun, and the teacher-turned-outlaw never had a fighting chance against the angry kid's furious onslaught.

Six rounds Billy put into the outlaw's body, and continued pulling the trigger until the girl brought him out of his trance. "He's dead, Mr. Bayes . . . for God's sake, he's dead. Now please untie me."

"I'm sorry, Miss Sanderson, I . . . I don't know whatever came over me."

"That's quite all right, Mr. Bayes. I understand—I really do. Those men were evil. If you hadn't gotten to them first, they would have killed us both. You were completely justified in what you did."

Removing the girl's ropes, Billy helped her to her feet, then caught her in his arms as she went limp.

"Miss Sanderson, are you going to be all right?"

"Please, just hold me in your arms a moment," she whispered.

Billy had no problem in complying with the girl's request; he had dreamed of holding her in his arms since the moment he first met her. Then, catching him by complete surprise, she kissed him full on the lips. For several minutes they embraced tightly, both reluctant to release the other. It was the girl who finally removed herself and said, "Your head's terribly bloody. You'd better come to the fire and let me have a look at it."

Back down to earth, Billy knelt beside Brogen's body and felt his pulse. "This one's a goner," he told Becky. "I must have hit him harder than I intended."

"He would've killed us both eventually, if you hadn't gotten him first."

"Yeah, I know," Billy said quietly, "but I had never taken a human life before I met this bunch. Killing a man is not something I take lightly. They forced me to do it."

Placing a consoling hand on Billy's shoulder, Becky said, "I understand, but you only did what you had to do, Mr. Bayes."

"Please, miss, would you mind calling me Billy?"

"I'd love to, but only if you call me Becky."

"I'd like that . . . Becky. Now, you mentioned something about looking at my head. Is the offer still open?"

"You know it is, Billy, but first I'd appreciate it if you would move that outlaw's body away from the fire. I don't think I can relax if I have to share it with him."

Hand in hand, they walked to the fire, where Billy took Fisk's body by the ankles and dragged him to the edge of the trees, positioning him next to Brogen. He then covered their bodies with their bedrolls and returned to the fire.

After boiling water in the coffeepot, Becky had Billy sit next to the fire, where she cleansed and inspected his head wound. "The bleeding has stopped, thankfully, but you're going to have a goose egg for a while yet,'' she said good-naturedly. ''How does it feel?''

''Like I was hit on the head with a rock,'' Billy replied. ''Now to more important things. Did they teach you to cook at that fancy finishing school?''

''Of course not, silly, it wasn't that kind of school. However, my Aunt Effie did teach me pretty much what I need to know to make do.''

Billy watched enraptured as Becky went about preparing a meal from the skimpy provisions taken from the outlaws' belongings. Never had he seen such graceful movements in a girl, and he was fairly bursting with his longing for her. He was in love, as he had known all along, but it was only now that he found himself willing to admit it to himself with any conviction.

And as of tonight, he was beginning to feel that she was equally in love with him. He had to pinch himself to make certain it was not all a dream. He'd had his doubts in the beginning whether she would even give him as much as a second look, but after the kiss earlier he realized they shared a mutual attraction.

''Why did you ride up alone?'' Billy asked her. ''You know your aunt is terribly worried about you.''

She stopped working the fire and brushed a strand of hair from her face. ''Why, I came looking for you, of course. What a silly question.''

''Why on earth would you come looking for me? I don't understand.''

''What's there to understand? I was responsible for your being out here in search of the Arabian, and I became worried when you didn't return after a couple of days. That day at the train depot . . . it wasn't your fault that the Arabian broke free and ran. The fact is, when you introduced yourself, I actually went weak and relaxed my grip on the lead rope.''

Billy grinned up at her and said, ''Then in a sense it was my fault the horse got away.''

''I suppose you could look at it that way. But tell me, did you ever catch up to the Arabian? With all the excitement it completely slipped my mind to ask.''

''Of course, he's stalled at the livery in Bent Rock—at least he was when I last saw him. The way my luck has been in trying to keep possession of that animal, I wouldn't be surprised if we find him gone again when we make it back to town.''

''I'm so relieved to hear he's finally back in Bent Rock. Father would disinherit me if I lost that horse.''

''What about yourself. How did you meet up with these owlhoots?''

''They came up on me unexpectedly while I was following the Arabian's tracks. I was watching the trail so intently that I didn't see them until they were right on me. When I tried to make a run for it, the chubby one, Fisk, chased me down and grabbed my reins.

''Then they brought me here to their camp and tied me to that tree where you first saw me. The older one, Brogen, asked me what I was doing out here, and I told them I was looking for you and the Arabian. At that, they just grinned and looked at each other like they knew something I didn't.''

''I'm sorry you had to go through all that,'' Billy said, taking her in his arms and holding her tenderly against his chest. ''They won't be bothering you again—ever.''

Chapter 9

After eating and tending the horses, Billy gathered arm-loads of juniper boughs in the darkness and carried them up the nearby talus and spread them on the ground beneath the protective cover of a large overhanging rock. Because of the incident with the Mexican bandits, he vowed that he would not be surprised in his sleep again. Using his bedroll and a couple of saddle blankets he made separate beds for Becky and himself, then joined her at the campfire, where she was making a pot of coffee.

"You didn't tell me how you came to know those two outlaws," Becky said, handing Billy a steaming cup of coffee. "From the way they had talked earlier, I assumed you'd had a confrontation with them in the past."

Billy blew on the hot coffee and tested it before answering the girl. "I guess you could say that. I was forced to shoot their partner last night."

"Shoot their partner? Maybe you should start from the beginning and tell me just what happened out there these past several days. You've been very busy, apparently."

"I suppose you can say I've been busy these past several days. But really, my experiences out there are not the sort a man would relate to a lady."

"Billy Bayes, how can it be much worse than what I was exposed to earlier in the evening. Lady or no, I want to

95

hear everything, beginning the moment you left Bent Rock in search of the Arabian—and don't spare me.''

Billy refilled his coffee cup and took a sip before relating his experiences on the trail, omitting nothing of his four-day adventure. As vivid as they were in his memory, he nevertheless had the feeling that he was telling the girl of experiences that had occurred in the far distant past. And as he went over it, detail by detail, he could not shake the notion that two of him had been out there on the trail, one as participant, the other as observer.

Ending his story with the blow to the head earlier in the evening, he sat silently and looked into Becky's eyes. Coming to Billy, she sat beside him and put her arm around his shoulders and said, ''I really had no idea, Billy. And it was all my fault for losing my grip on the Arabian's lead rope. Can you ever forgive me?''

''What's to forgive? The most of what I went through these past four days I brought on myself. I can truthfully say my troubles began with the Mexican bandits—which was entirely my fault.''

''Still, you had a relatively trouble-free life until I showed up. Don't deny it, Billy.''

''Maybe so, Becky, but finding you made everything I went through worth the trouble, believe me.''

''Why, that's about the sweetest thing anyone has ever said to me, Billy.''

''Really? I'm sure those fancy city boys back in Baltimore said as much when they courted you.''

''What boys? You're the first boy I've ever been alone with. My aunt had always insisted on chaperoning me whenever I socialized.

''And what about you, Billy, I'll just bet you've known many girls, haven't you?''

"That's a real laugh. Aren't too many females out on the range, you know."

"I realize that, but as I remember they had those dances every Saturday night in Sayers Flat. They still do, don't they?"

"Nothing but spoiled ranchers' daughters at those shindigs. Heck, girls like that don't hardly look at an ordinary cowhand."

"Well, I like that! Some would consider me a spoiled rancher's daughter—or haven't you heard?"

"You? Headstrong maybe—but spoiled? I think not."

Later, lying on their separate bedrolls, both Billy and Becky were too excited by the day's happenings to sleep. Neither was aware of the other's restlessness as they stared into the night and thought over the recent events that had brought them together.

Billy knew he was truly in love with the beautiful daughter of his employer. He could think of no other girl with whom he would rather spend the rest of his life. But what could possibly come of such a union? She was the only child of a wealthy rancher, a girl accustomed to all the finer things in life that only money and breeding could provide.

And what was he? The drifting son of a Kansas sodbuster, without either family or breeding, without money or a formal education.

Young and in love, they could make it without money in the beginning; young love has a way of making one immune to poverty. But what about later, when they began to grow into maturity. Would love alone be enough then?

He thought not. It was foolish of him to even imagine that he, Billy Bayes, could possibly possess the eternal love of a girl like Becky Sanderson without making something of himself; their stations in life were just too different.

And how would her father react when he found out that his daughter was in love with one of his young hired hands. That he might be sent packing, Billy could well imagine.

Becky could not sleep either, for thinking about Billy. She was inexplicably drawn to this handsome boy who seemed to carry himself like a man, a boy who had been forced by the circumstances of birth and environment to mature beyond his years. There was something magnetic in the way she was attracted to him.

Never, since being sent back East after her mother had passed away, had she met such a boy as Billy. Having attended an all-girl school in Baltimore, the only boys with whom she came in contact were the pampered sons of elite families.

She needed the strength of someone like Billy, for she herself was possessed of a pioneer spirit that traced its roots to those early years on the Rocking J, when her family was struggling to carve an empire out of a wasteland that yielded only to persistent courage and dogged determination.

Throughout her years living in Baltimore, she had felt like a displaced person, living a temporary existence in anticipation of returning to the vast, open country that was so much a part of her.

As she grew toward maturity, she had formed a vague mental image of the caliber of man it would take to complement her own strong will, and from the moment she first met Billy, the once vague image began to take form and substance in her mind. She did not doubt that she had finally found her true love.

And as she thought about him, the distance between their bedrolls became too great for her, and she got to her feet and spread her blanket over Billy and crawled underneath it.

Billy had barely nodded off when he felt the additional blanket cover his body, followed by the warm body of Becky snuggling against him. Embracing her tenderly, he kissed her lightly on the tip of her nose, then full on her lips. This had to be a dream, he told himself. No man was entitled to this much happiness in real life.

At first light, Billy crawled from under Becky's embrace without disturbing her sleep and began gathering wood for a breakfast fire. He felt better than he had felt in ages, and went about his chore whistling softly in contentment. From time to time he looked up to where the girl lay sleeping, and he would feel an onrush of love that virtually made his spirit soar. Never had he felt this much love for another human being.

After getting a good fire going and the coffee boiling, Billy crossed the little stream to where the horses had been hobbled throughout the night, intending to water them in preparation for the trip into Bent Rock. At once he noticed one of the horses was missing, a sorrel belonging to one of the outlaws.

In his discomfiture, Billy rounded up the remaining horses and removed their hobbles and led them to the stream. He had counted on the two extra mounts to carry the bodies of the outlaws to town to turn over to the local marshal there. Now, he would have to somehow make one horse do the job. Apparently, he figured, the missing horse had lost its hobble during the night and wandered off, but he wasn't about to go looking for him; he'd had enough of that with the Arabian.

The three horses watered, Billy cinched their saddles and walked a pair of them to the thicket where the blanket-covered bodies of the outlaws lay, but to his utter surprise one of the bodies was missing. Lifting the blanket that covered the one corpse, he verified it to be that of Fisk. Brogen was missing.

Frantically searching the surrounding area, Billy found no sign of the outlaw, and finally concluded that the man had not been killed by the blow he had dealt him, as he had first thought, and, without either saddle or gun, it appeared, Brogen had ridden off sometime during the night.

Deciding against remaining in camp long enough to cook breakfast, Billy climbed up the incline to where Becky still lay sleeping. Shaking her awake, they embraced tightly. Neither spoke for a moment, and it was he who finally broke the mood. "Brogen is gone, along with one of the horses. I think we'd better clear out of here right away."

"Gone? How is that possible? I thought . . . ''

"Yeah, I thought so too. I even checked his pulse last night, and there wasn't one. That man seems to have nine lives. Real spooky, isn't it?''

"Very. What're we going to do now?''

"I'm all saddled up and ready to move out whenever you are. I, for one, am ready to get back to town. There's been too much happening out here to suit me, and the sooner I get you back to civilization the better I'll feel," Billy said.

"I must look a mess, but I'm ready to leave."

Having broke camp earlier, Billy took his bedroll and led Becky down to where the saddled horses were waiting. Fisk's body he had slung over the saddle and tied securely in place, along with a small arsenal of rifles and six-guns belonging to the outlaws.

They left the campsite at a brisk trot, both Billy and Becky anxious to put it behind them. And although they were leaving behind them some bad memories of their ordeal at the hands of the outlaws, the good memories would remain with them for many years, and they would always look back at that night with much emotion.

On the trail, Billy's thoughts kept returning to Brogen. The man was like a bad dream that returned night after night, just when you thought you were shut of it. Would he run across the outlaw again—at a time when he least expected to see him? Billy didn't think so; even if Brogen had managed to survive the blow to his head, he shouldn't be all that anxious to confront a mere boy who had twice managed to get the best of him.

The way Billy had it figured, the man had ridden off in a daze from his head wound. Why else did he fail to saddle his horse, or arm himself, or run off the remaining horses and strand them there? A man in his right mind would have done all those things. Chances were, he was lying dead on the trail somewhere, having finally given in to his wound.

It was well past the noon hour when the trail-weary couple finally reached downtown Bent Rock, and the blanket-draped body lying across the saddle attracted much attention as they made their way down the crowded street toward the marshal's office. And by the time they made it to the town square, they had at least a dozen townsmen following them on horseback and on foot.

Several in the crowd could no longer contain their curiosity when Billy tied up in front of the marshall's office, and they lifted the blanket and studied the outlaw's face.

"Well, I don't know him," one idler said, aiming a spatshot at the horse's hoof and wiping the dribble from his chin. "Wonder who he be?"

"I reckon he's not from these parts," offered another.

"Dang if he don't look familiar," said one old-timer, scratching his head reflectively, "but I can't place him right off."

Boyd Michaud, the United States marshal for the district, was an amiable man who listened with professional interest to Billy's detailed account of his run-in with the bandits and outlaws. He related to the marshal his experiences of the last several days, pointing out locations on a map tacked to the office wall, including where he might find Beak's body.

"You should have come in and told me about that shooting right after it happened, Bayes. But I can understand how it was kind of early when you came back to town yesterday morning. If you had talked to me before you rode out again, I might have saved you and the young lady the ordeal you had to go through last night. That's my job. That's what I'm here for."

"I was just too tired to think about it, marshal. All I could think about was getting myself some shut-eye."

"Well, son, I can understand that. Now, about those three owlhoots. From the names you gave me, I'd say you had yourself a couple of run-ins with the old Brogen gang.

"That Brogen gang was a thorn in my side from the very day I pinned on my badge, but that was a long time ago. These days, there's too much law for that kind to operate like they once did. The gang just sort of broke up and scattered over the years, until there wasn't much left of them but several over-the-hill types who resigned themselves to rustling a steer of two just to survive.

"The three you said you encountered, Brogen, Fisk, and Beak, were the remnants of a gang that once numbered fifteen, maybe twenty men. Oh, they were good, too. They hit trains, banks, stagecoaches—most anything where big money was involved, then they would just disappear into the mountains. We were never able to pinpoint their hideout and shake them out of those hills.

"Over the last years, they were into small-time stuff.

Mostly they would combine forces with some renegade Kiowas and rustle a few head of cattle from the ranchers in the area. They were smart enough to take only a few head from each ranch they hit—just enough to keep from upsetting the balance and causing folks to go looking for them. The ranchers only wrote off their losses as a necessary operating expense.''

"What about the man outside, marshal. You know much about him?" Billy asked.

"Fisk? Yeah, supposedly he's an educated man, turned outlaw—from back East. Seems he had an insatiable craving for female flesh—younger the better. According to the reward dodgers I have on file, there's still an outstanding reward for his capture, dead or alive, put up by some influential bigwig back in New York. Seems this Fisk had his way with the man's young daughter, then made his way out here and joined up with Brogen's bunch.

"I'd have to go through some old wanted posters, but I believe there have been rewards offered for his capture by the railroad and stage lines he robbed over the years. Seems there were at least eighteen shootings attributed to that gang in the course of their crimes.

"Now, take this owlhoot you said you shot up in the mountains, fellow calls himself Beak. He was a dangerous man if ever there was one. Shoot a man just for looking at him in the wrong way. Why, there's been more than a dozen shootings attributed to his guns alone, and that's only the ones we know about. Still was a substantial reward out for him, last I checked.

"All in all, I'd say you did a service to the citizens of New Mexico and the surrounding states, and once I take a couple of deputies to that hideout you pointed out on the map, and verify Beak's corpse, you should have made yourself quite a bit of reward money.

"Now, let's go outside and have a look-see at that jasper you brought in—to verify his identity for the records, you understand."

The marshal made a path through the curious crowd that had gotten larger while Billy and Becky were in his office, and pulled back the blanket and studied the face at length. "Yeah, that's him all right. That's Fisk; I recognize his features from the wanted flyers. Guess we can scratch him off the books."

"Are you about finished with us, marshal? Miss Sanderson and I should let her aunt know she's back. I imagine she's worried about her, being gone since yesterday morning."

"Sure, I reckon I have about all the information I'll need, Bayes. Whatever comes of the reward money on those jaspers, I'll be contacting the marshal up in Sayers Flat. As for Brogen, I wouldn't worry too much about him if I were you. From what you told me, I expect we'll find him stretched out on the trail somewheres."

"Thanks, marshal. We'll be staying at the Tivoli Hotel for the next couple of days, should you need us for anything."

Chapter 10

Becky dismounted in front of the hotel and handed her reins to Billy and said, "I'd better let Auntie know we're back. I imagine she's beside herself with worry by now. And you will join us for dinner this evening, won't you?"

"Just you try and keep me away," Billy said, looking down at her.

Lowering her voice, Becky said, "Billy, I haven't said it yet, but I love you . . . I'll always love you. And I'll always remember last night."

"I love you too, Becky . . . loved you from the start, but it took last night to make me realize just how much."

At the livery stable, Billy returned the rental horses and checked on the Arabian and chestnut and bay. They all appeared well-rested and in good condition. Rubbing the chestnut's nose affectionately, Billy said, "I'll bet you're ready to get back to the Rocking J, aren't you, boy? I sure as shooting know I am. A cowboy can get himself into one awful mess when he's on vacation."

Billy ordered hot water for his room and soaked the trail dust and dried blood and perspiration from his pores, then he shaved and donned his remaining clean shirt and denim pants. Feeling like a new man, he walked down the hallway and knocked on Effie Sanderson's door. She had earlier left a note that she wished to speak with him.

"Why, Mr. Bayes, do come in. I have just ordered up

a pot of tea. Please be seated and make yourself comfortable.''

''Thank you, ma'am,'' Billy said, taking a seat.

''I had a talk with my niece earlier this evening, and she told me of your ordeal on the trail. Mr. Bayes, I had no idea. How are your wounds? I shall have a physician check you out, if you wish.''

''That's hardly necessary, ma'am, but thanks anyway. A person gets use to knocks and bruises out on the range. Besides, I'm a mighty fast healer, and I'll be just fine.''

''As you wish, Mr. Bayes, but I feel just awful. After all, we did send you out after that horse, and I feel somewhat responsible.''

''Don't let it bother you, ma'am. It's done and over with.''

''Well, I suppose things do have a way of working out for the best—at least that has always been my philosophy. But I must say, you look much better at this moment than you did yesterday morning.''

The conversation was interrupted by a knock on the door, and the woman excused herself and admitted a uniformed maid who curtsied and set a tray on the table in front of them.

Pouring steaming tea into a small, fragile-looking cup, Effie Sanderson said, ''Do you take sugar, Mr. Bayes?''

''No, ma'am, just cream, please.''

''Now, Mr. Bayes, there is a matter of the strictest confidence that we must discuss between us. I would rather hope that what I am about to say will be kept from my niece. May I depend on you to keep this conversation confidential?''

''I guess so, ma'am . . . ''

"Dear me, this is rather delicate, Mr. Bayes, so how to begin—"

"Excuse me for interrupting, ma'am, but whatever it is you're trying to tell me, it's probably better if you just get to the point. You don't have to spare me."

"Yes, you're quite right. Mr. Bayes, you and my niece are both young, unmarried adults, and you can just imagine the speculation that could result from your having spent the night together in the mountains last night—"

"But, ma'am—"

"I realize that it was because of circumstances not of your choosing that you had to remain overnight in the mountains," she said, waving away his interruption impatiently. "It was understandably unavoidable, and I think the three of us are in complete agreement on that point."

"If everybody agrees that we had to stay out there because of the dark, then what is your point, ma'am?"

"It is not we who will take it the wrong way, Mr. Bayes; it is perhaps others that we must worry about, people who are less understanding than the three of us."

"What others? Look, your niece and I were taken prisoners by a gang of desperados who meant to do us mortal harm, and it was only through pure luck we came out of it in one piece. And you're worried about what folks will think? Ma'am, if you don't beat all."

"Please try and control your temper, Mr. Bayes. There are certain things you do not know about my brother. I should not be telling you this, but as long as we are speaking in confidence, I may as well let it out. There are plans in the making to put my brother up for the nomination of governor when the territory becomes a state.

"Can you understand how talk of his daughter having

spent the night alone with one of his hired hands could adversely affect his chances of winning that office?

"Politics is a very dirty business, Mr. Bayes, and the opposition will go to great lengths to smear the name of this family, just for their own gain. It is the way of politics in this country.

"Image is everything, and my brother has a spotless reputation among both his friends and his potential rivals, and I would hate to see his ambitions crushed by idle talk concerning his daughter and one of his employees. Many very promising careers have been dashed for less reasons. But we will not give my brother's political adversaries reason for idle gossip, will we, Mr. Bayes?"

"No, of course not, ma'am, but I don't have the damndest notion what you're talking about. Are you telling me that spending the night out there with your niece was so terribly wrong?"

Now it was Effie Sanderson's turn to lose her temper. "What I have been saying, Mr. Bayes, is that *last night never happened*, and my niece never once left this hotel without my having chaperoned her. Now, my good sir, is *that* perfectly clear enough for your understanding?"

Billy smiled slightly at the woman's last statement, knowing that what he was about to drop on her would undoubtedly put her at loose ends with herself. "Clear to me, yes, but there's something you have to be made aware of, ma'am. You see, earlier this afternoon your niece and I filed an official report of the incident up there with the district United States marshal here in Bent Rock. The fact we spent the night out there together is now public record."

"Oh, dear," she said, fingering her collar nervously. "My niece failed to mention it. This can be complicating . . . "

"Look, ma'am, I hardly know you at all, and until a few minutes ago we've not passed more than a few words between us. But I do know your brother—have for nigh on to four years—and I know him to be a straight shooter. With all due respect, ma'am, I think you underestimate your own brother.

"And concerning the matter of Becky and me, I'll be honest in admitting that we have developed some feelings for each other, and I plan to ask her father's permission to court her when I see him."

"*You*? A common ranch hand . . . courting my niece? Over my dead body, Mr. Bayes. What could you, an uneducated, penniless cowboy possibly offer a refined girl like Rebecca? Why, she has been personally groomed by me, her only aunt, for the very best life has to offer, and that, my dear sir, does not include marrying a man beneath her station."

"I don't believe there was any mention of marrying any time soon, ma'am. I only said I plan to court her. We're young yet, and there's plenty of time to be talking about a future together."

"And just how do you plan to make a future for yourself, Mr. Bayes, a future that would provide you with the means by which to support my niece in the manner to which she is accustomed? I would certainly like to hear it from you."

"Ma'am," Billy replied defensively, "your brother came to this country at about my age and I have it by good account that he hardly had more than two cents to rub together. He made it from the back of a horse, just like I intend to make it from the back of a horse. I think that is something your brother can relate to."

"Do you also have it by good account, Mr. Bayes, that by the time my brother made it, as you say, his poor wife had fallen victim to the consumption brought on by the hardships of those early years of struggle? Yes, indeed! By the time my brother had made something of the Rocking J, his wife was no longer around to enjoy the fruits of her many years of labor.

"And poor Rebecca. She was only nine years old when her mother passed away. Think what the child has missed by not having her mother around while she was growing up. It is sad to say, but it always seems to be the woman who must pay the supreme sacrifice in this country.

"But not Rebecca, not while I have a living breath in my body. I will not stand idly by and let all her advantages go to blazes, just because you think you're in love with her. What happened to her poor mother will not be wished on my niece."

"I hardly see how you can make a comparison, ma'am. Times have changed since back then, and it wouldn't be like that at all. I'm sorry about her mother, I truly am, but it doesn't make sense for you to think that Becky would end up like her mother."

"Mr. Bayes, I do not wish to prolong this conversation. I can see that it is getting us nowhere. And until we leave Bent Rock, two days hence, you will not speak to my niece, and you will not join us for meals. You, my dear sir, are a hired hand, and you must keep your station in mind. Do I make myself perfectly clear on that?"

"That you do, ma'am."

"Then good day, sir. We have nothing more to discuss."

"I guess not, ma'am."

Well, well, Billy thought, that certainly puts me in my place. That the woman had reminded him that he was a hireling now weighed heavily on his mind. Just his rotten luck he had to fall in love with the daughter of his employer.

Let Effie Sanderson think what she would, Billy thought. She didn't realize the stuff that William Charles Bayes was made of, but he knew, and no way was he going to let her prejudices come between him and the girl he loved.

He would comply with Effie Sanderson's demands and stay away from her niece when she was around, but in direct defiance of the the aunt, he would see Becky at the time and place of his own choosing. The woman just did not understand the power of love.

Billy could not very well eat in the same hotel dining room as Becky and not share her table. To do so would be an obvious slight, and he could not do that to her. She would just have to wonder about his absence until he could find a chance to get her alone and explain the situation to her.

Finding a little Mexican restaurant down the street, Billy dined alone, and even though he liked most all Mexican food, he found it to be tasteless in this instance. It wasn't bad fare, as Mexican food went, it was just that eating alone after looking forward to dining with Becky left him more than a little melancholy. If this was how it was going to be all the way back to the Rocking J, he had a miserable trip in front of him.

Leaving most of the food still on his plate, Billy walked down the street to the livery stable and checked on the horses. Borrowing a brush from the stableboy, he joined the chestnut in his stall and began to curry him, letting his thoughts run free.

Effie Sanderson's words still rang in his ears. Maybe she was right about his station in life. Perhaps it was time to ponder somebody else's point of view other than his own. After all, what could he offer Becky, other than himself, that she did not have, or could not obtain with her father's money and influence?

But what of himself? He had never had reason to look past the weekly dances in Sayers Flat, much less what he would be doing next year—or the years following. The stark reality was that he had no dreams or ambitions other than being the best cowboy that he could possibly be. The aunt was right about him; he was just a complacent ranch hand, nothing more.

However, Billy thought, he was only nineteen years old, and he had plenty of time in which to start planning a future for himself, one that would also include Becky. They were both young yet and had their entire lives in front of them.

He could see no reason why he couldn't figure out a way to leave Sanderson's payroll and strike out on his own. He would have to do just that to keep his pride intact and maintain Becky's respect.

He would discuss it with old Josh when he got back to the ranch. He had often mentioned finding himself a small spread up north of the Canadian, where a man could still find good grazing for a small herd, and where the land was selling cheap. Maybe together they could form a partnership of sorts, with Josh putting up the money and him providing the labor.

Although, at the moment, he had no real definite plans for the future, Billy felt that his thinking process had been jarred into action by the practical Effie Sanderson, and he was at last beginning to think in terms of the possibility of making something of himself, and to him that was a positive first step.

Chapter 11

Billy pulled the buckboard to a stop in front of the Tivoli Hotel and loaded the trunks and bags. He had never seen the likes of such luggage, but it was understandable that Becky was returning to the Rocking J with an accumulation of nine years. Not only had she a large wardrobe and all those personal things that women think are absolutely necessary to daily living, she had brought with her all her favorite books. And there were her aunt's belongings, enough to carry her through the entire summer—and then some. And there was the added weight of the clothing they had purchased in Bent Rock, clothing considered more suitable for Western living than the stylish frocks they had brought with them from back East.

All that luggage was fine with Billy, but he was concerned about the tremendous strain on the light buckboard. Although it was built to withstand the bumps and grinds of the rocky terrain, there was a limit to how much weight could be safely placed on the axles.

Then there was the big bay horse that had to pull all the weight. That he was a sturdy animal, Billy had no doubt, but he would be put to the ultimate test before this trip would be over.

Billy only hoped that the next couple of days would go smoothly for him. He'd had more problems in the last several days than the average cowboy could expect in an entire lifetime.

He assisted the ladies aboard the rig, and was reassured by the warmth of Becky's hand on his shoulder as she placed it there for balance. Yet, he could see the deep hurt in her pleading green eyes as they momentarily met his, and he knew the hurt was there as the result of his having avoided her for the past two days.

He wanted to take her in his arms and tell her that nothing had changed between them since that night in the hills, but he knew it would be difficult to get her alone to express to her how he really felt about her. Her aunt would be watching them like a hawk from here on end, both on the long trail and back at the ranch. He would just abide his time until that inevitable moment when the older woman would slip up and let her guard down.

Billy felt that it would better serve their interest if he pretended to ignore Becky's presence until an opportune time presented itself—a time when the older woman was otherwise occupied.

Handing the bay's reins to Becky without an exchange of words, Billy mounted the waiting chestnut and took the lead out of town. If all went as planned, they could expect to be in Las Cumbres by early evening. If it were just he and the chestnut making the trip, Billy calculated, he could cut across country and arrive at the ranch sometime late that very night.

Riding some distance behind Billy, Becky was inwardly proud of the way he sat the saddle. Unlike most men who spent time on a horse, his body did not have the drooping shoulders and bent back, and to her, it seemed, there existed a silent communication between him and the chestnut, as though the horse's subtle movements were telegraphed to the rider.

Thinking of Billy, a sadness came over her, followed by an inexplicable feeling of having lost something of great personal value, something that had come to be hers only after having waited a lifetime to find.

They were soul mates, of this she had no doubt whatsoever, but since that early afternoon when he had dropped her off in front of the hotel, he had been avoiding her. She could not understand why he was so cold and distant this morning when he helped her aboard the wagon. Her mind raced back to that afternoon when they had returned from the mountains, and she could think of nothing she did or said that could have turned him off so abruptly.

Could it be that he had faked his feelings for her up in the mountains that night? It was possible. She had overheard girls talking about boys, who, once they had a girl on an intimate basis, dropped them for girls who were not so free with their affections. Did she err in joining him in his bedroll that night like some cheap harlot? Yes, she thought sadly, perhaps he now regarded her as just another roll in the hay, a tryst not to be taken seriously—but somehow she doubted it.

But how could he, she wondered, just cut it off like they had meant nothing to each other—without so much as an explanation? He had felt the same feelings as she had experienced at the camp that night, of that she had no doubts; there are some things a woman just knows intuitively, and accepts as a fact. No one, not even the best actor in the world is capable of exhibiting the feeling he shared with her that night without it meaning something deep and lasting.

Whatever the reason he had been avoiding her, she would

extract it from him when she found the opportunity. What she felt for him was much too profound to shrug off as a lark.

Effie Sanderson also admired the impressive way Billy sat the saddle. She had to admit, as well, that he was every bit as handsome as her niece had said. Also, she was secretly impressed by the way he had handled that gang of ruffians who had kidnapped and attempted to harm her niece. He had, after all, saved her from a fate worse than death—if not from death itself, for all anyone knew. For that, at least, she owed him a debt of gratitude for his intervention.

He and her niece would make such a lovely couple, no doubt, and he would probably make her a good husband. But he seemed totally lacking in ambition, a fact which grated on her. He was an ordinary cowboy, and he would remain so for the duration of his life, of that fact she had no reservations, and that was not nearly good enough for the niece whom she had personally groomed for a better life. A better future awaited her niece, and that future had no room for the likes of Billy Bayes.

Once out of Bent Rock, Billy reined over to the side of the road and allowed the buckboard with the trailing Arabian to get ahead of him. His move was partly meant to prevent stirring up dust that might settle on the ladies, but, for the most part, his motive for riding behind the buckboard was selfish. He missed Becky and wanted to be in a position to look at her unobserved.

How self-assured she appeared with the reins in her hands, Billy thought. Although she possessed the poise of a girl of breeding, she could also be strong and self-reliant, and he figured she could do just about anything she had to do to make it in this wild country. And in spite of her wealth and finishing school education, she was more like himself in more ways than he cared to think about. Together, he figured, they could eventually build their own empire in an unsettled part of the state, and do it without help.

Coming to a way station between Bent Rock and Las Cumbres, Billy watered the horses and checked out the buckboard while the ladies freshened up from their arduous trip before eating lunch.

After taking care of the horses, Billy entered the dining room to join the ladies, but was waved off by the defiant expression given him by Effie Sanderson. Apparently he was not welcome to join them, so he took his plate and ate alone on the attached patio.

Leaving the way station an hour later, Billy again took the lead to check out rocks and holes in advance of the buckboard. From this point on, the condition of the road went from bad to worse.

It was early spring and the countryside was alive with the many colors of wildflowers. Billy had an overpowering urge to stop and pick a bouquet for Becky, but he didn't wish to risk the ire of her stern-visaged aunt who rode beside her, aloof and indifferent to the beautiful countryside through which they rode.

The remainder of the trip into Las Cumbres, their midway point to the ranch, was, for the most part, uneventful, and by the time they arrived there in the early evening, Billy was tired of traveling and ready to put his feet on the ground.

He unloaded the buckboard at the only hotel in town and took the rig and horses to the livery down the street. After tending the animals and making arrangements for having the wagon axles greased, he made his way back to the hotel and prepared for dinner.

Not having bath facilities readily available, Billy splashed water on his face and shaved from the pitcher of water and bowl provided with his room. He debated whether to eat in the hotel dining room or search out another restaurant in the one-horse town. He was too hungry to go without eating, yet he didn't want to share the same dining room with Becky and have to eat alone.

As he debated his eating arrangements, someone knocked timidly on his door. Having had a bad run of luck lately in regard to strangers, Billy loosened the leather thong from the hammer of his six-gun and cracked the door part of the way. Appearing uncertain of herself, Becky was about to turn away when he opened the door wider and grinned at her.

"Becky," he merely said, surprised to find her at his door while he was thinking about her.

"Billy . . . I hope I'm not intruding, but we really must talk while Auntie isn't around. Would you think it too improper of me if we talked in your room?"

"Not this old boy. Please . . . come in."

"Thank you. Now would you mind closing the door— just in case Auntie happens to walk past."

She refused the offered chair and sat on the bed instead. Looking at him confidently, she said, "I want to know why you've been avoiding me these past several days. You can't deny you haven't. I'm in love with you, Billy, and I thought you loved me as well. Don't you think I'm at least due the courtesy of an explanation?"

"Didn't your aunt talk to you about us?"

"No, not really. Is there some reason why she should have? The only time your name came up was on that night back in Bent Rock when you failed to show up for dinner as you had promised. I asked Auntie if she had any idea why you didn't dine with us, and she only shrugged and said that it was likely you were too self-conscious to join us—you being only a hired-hand. I remember telling her I didn't think that was the case at all. She ignored that and began talking about something irrelevant.''

"Becky, I find this difficult to discuss, knowing how close you are to your aunt. I wouldn't want to say anything that would put her in a bad light—''

"You had better tell me, Billy," she interrupted. "It's beginning to come clear to me now. She said something to you, and I adamantly refuse to leave this room until I learn the truth.''

"Please, Becky, I don't want to be the one to come between you and your aunt. She was probably right, after all.''

"Right about what? Did my aunt tell you to stay away from me? That's it! I can see it in your eyes.''

"I promised your aunt I wouldn't tell you what we discussed that night back in Bent Rock.''

"For the last time, Billy, what did she say?''

"Well . . . I do feel that she intimidated me that night, if you want the truth of the matter.''

"For the last time, Billy, what did she say to you?''

"You won't hold it against her if I say?''

"I won't hold it against her. Now tell me.''

"Well, in a few words, she said you can do much better than me, that you deserve someone with higher ambitions. She's right of course. I've been much too complacent as a hired-hand.

"All that'll change, now that she has me thinking seriously about the future, but as it stands presently, I don't have a dang thing to offer a girl like you, and that's the truth of it, Becky.''

"Billy Bayes, how can you stand there and say you have nothing to offer me. You have yourself, and that *is* everything. If two people love each other, everything else will come in due time.''

''It's not what we believe. It's what your aunt believes, and I suppose she's entitled to that. After all, she did raise you, partly, and she's only concerned about your welfare. Truth is, I admire her in a way for saying how she feels about me. If nothing else comes from our discussion, she certainly got me to thinking.''

''Thinking about what, Billy?''

''Me . . . us. That talk with her jarred me into considering the future—something I never did before. I've been thinking about looking into some open range up north of the Canadian. It'll be mighty rough starting out from scratch, but I'm young yet, and there isn't a thing I don't know about ranching. I just know I can make it on my own.''

''Why, of course you can, Billy. I have faith in you, and I know you can do anything you set your mind to. But tell me, are you planning to do it . . . alone?''

''In the beginning, yes. But a man like me will eventually need the companionship of a good woman. Know anybody like that?''

''Oh, could be I know just the one. She was partly reared on a ranch herself, and she has this country in her blood. Shall I tell her you'll be coming back for her?''

''You can tell her it's a promise.''

''She'll be counting the days.''

''Now tell me, Becky Sanderson, just how in the blazes did you come to be in my room without your aunt shadowing you?''

''We're having to share the same room, and she wanted to be alone to freshen up. She's extremely modest, you know.''

"You're joshing. I never would have suspected," Billy laughed.

"Oh, it's so good to hear you laughing again, Billy. I've missed that in you these past several days. Now I have to go before Auntie comes looking for me. But promise me you'll join us for dinner in a few minutes. If Auntie happens to remark about it, just pay her no mind. Now promise me you'll join us this time."

"I'll be there, depend on it. Tell me, though, have you ever been kissed in a man's hotel room?"

"And what if I haven't, am I about to be?"

As Billy had promised, he walked into the hotel dining room moments behind the Sanderson ladies and pulled out a chair and seated himself next to Becky.

"Auntie, I asked Mr. Bayes to join us for dinner. It must have completely slipped my mind to tell you earlier," Becky said with a straight face.

"How nice," the older woman said, but in a tight little voice that sounded both forced and insincere.

Knowing Effie Sanderson as he was now beginning to, Billy didn't believe she would let show in public her true feelings about the unexpected change in the dining arrangements, and on the surface he pretended that his presence at her table was an accepted fact.

And not the one to let the occasion go by without making the best of it, Billy regaled Becky with anecdotes of life on the range and in the bunkhouse back at the Rocking J, and even the older woman forgot her reserve at times and joined in the laughter.

"Mr. Bayes," Becky addressed him formally when the waiter brought the menus, "you stated you had eaten here previously, so perhaps you can recommend an entree from the menu. I shall order the same as you—if you do not mind.''

"Very well, Miss Sanderson, I was considering their broiled buffalo tongue, followed by—"

"Buffalo tongue? Buffalo tongue?"

"Please, Auntie, you are repeating yourself again," Becky said. Addressing herself to Billy she said, "You must forgive my aunt, Mr. Bayes. Her age, you know."

"Do not be impertinent, Rebecca. Besides, civilized people do not eat the tongues of wild beasts, particularly of beasts as disgustingly ugly as the buffalo."

"Begging to differ with you, ma'am," Billy said, "but buffalo tongue has been on the menus of the finest restaurants in the East for years now. I would be very surprised if you told me you'd not had the pleasure of trying it."

"Then you may consider yourself surprised, young man, for I have not eaten of it, nor do I intend to do so now."

"I don't know, ma'am, but one day soon I expect to see the buffalo extinct, and when that happens, you'll probably kick yourself for not having tried it here tonight."

"Mr. Bayes, if I decline to eat the tongue of the buffalo, I can rest assured that I shall have done my part in prolonging that inevitable day when the poor animal is *declared* extinct."

"Poor Auntie," Becky said, taking her hand. "Mr. Bayes was only having fun. Of course they don't have buffalo tongue on the menu."

"Sure they do, Miss Sanderson, and that's what I'm having for dinner. You're going to try it, aren't you?"

"Ugh, I'm with Auntie. I think I'll pass on the buffalo tongue this time."

After a pleasant meal, Billy escorted the ladies to the door of their hotel room and wished them a good night.

The evening had passed with hardly a discordant note, leaving him feeling that maybe Effie Sanderson's tough reserve could be broached with time and patience. He certainly hoped so, as he needed an ally in her if he hoped to pursue his plans to court her niece.

Preparing herself for bed, Effie Sanderson said, "You know, Rebecca, that young man can be quite charming for a cowboy. I must say I actually enjoyed his presence at dinner tonight. And he is much more intelligent and articulate than I had earlier given him credit for. Who would have thought it—in this wilderness."

"My goodness, Auntie, how you do go on. My father lives in this so-called wilderness. Do you find him any less intelligent for doing so? For that matter, I was born in this wilderness, and I certainly don't believe that makes me any less intelligent."

"You and your father? What a ridiculous comparison, Rebecca. You both came from good Baltimore stock in the beginning, and that does not compare to that young man. Besides, just look at what your father has accomplished since he first arrived in this country."

"And what makes you think Mr. Bayes—Billy—does not come from good stock, Auntie? Surely you aren't judging him by the singular fact that he works for my Father. You seem to forget that Father also worked as a hired hand when he first arrived here nearly thirty years ago. Don't you see it, Auntie? Billy is no different than Father was back then. He merely needs time, that's all."

"Now that is exactly my point, Rebecca—time. Your father spent many years preparing a good life for you, and it bears repeating that your mother paid the ultimate price for the success of the Rocking J, and for what? So your life would be less filled with the hardships they had to endure.

In a large sense they paid your dues for you. Why do you wish to tie yourself to someone just starting out from scratch, when it has already been obtained for you?''

"Now that Father is successful, I must become the spoiled daughter of a wealthy rancher. Is that what you're trying to tell me? Well, I am my father's daughter all right, and I have the same pioneer spirit in my blood. Just as my father did, I'd like to become a part of this country, but not by sitting around and hosting teas for other spoiled ladies. This is a growing country yet, and I feel inclined to make my contribution to its growth in other ways.''

"What other way is there, Rebecca? Why, you're talking pure gibberish.''

"Call it what you will, Auntie, but if Billy will have me, I'll defy both you and Father to try and stop me from some-day marrying him and spending the rest of my life with him. You've said he's not good enough for me. Well, I only hope that I'm good enough for him. Don't you think you can open your mind just a little where Billy is con-cerned—for my sake?''

"Oh, do not confuse an old lady. I do not know what I think anymore. A person spends her entire life learning values, then along comes a situation that makes it all so meaningless. I am not really in a position to stop you from doing what you think is right, but as one who loves you and is concerned for your future happiness and welfare, I can only advise you to discuss your feelings with your father before you pursue this any further. Perhaps he can talk some sense into you. I have washed my hands of it.''

"Then nothing has changed, has it? You still don't think Billy an acceptable suitor for me?''

"What I think is of little importance, Rebecca. As I have

previously stated, this is something that you and your father will have to discuss between you. As far as I am concerned, it is out of my hands. What is more, I do not wish to discuss it any further.''

Chapter 12

Up and about the next morning, Billy's first concern was the buckboard. The trail between Las Cumbres and the Rocking J was nothing more than a couple of deep ruts, with potholes and rocks waiting to shear an axle or damage a wheel. As rough as he had found the road on his earlier trip with the empty buckboard, he could just imagine what the road would do to a loaded wagon—and with the ladies at the reins, to boot.

The man at the livery had done a thorough job of greasing the axles, and that helped to ease Billy's mind somewhat, but there still remained the worry of all that luggage. He dared not suggest that some of the heavier trunks, such as books, be stored in Las Cumbres until a later time when another wagon could be sent to pick them up and haul them to the ranch. Even for him to hint at leaving something behind, he surmised, would most likely put him at greater odds with Effie Sanderson. The woman could be very unreasonable when she wanted to be, and the uneasy truce they had mutually acquiesced to at dinner last evening was not a thing he wished to disrupt midway through their trip.

Hitching the bay to the buckboard and saddling the chestnut, Billy tied the Arabian to the wagon and walked all the horses the short distance to the front of the hotel, where he loaded the waiting luggage.

To his surprise, the ladies were already dressed for the

road and just finishing their breakfast when Billy entered the hotel dining room. A smiling Becky motioned for him to join them while they finished their coffee.

"Well, ladies," Billy said, "looks like your next breakfast will be eaten at the Rocking J."

"I can hardly believe I shall actually be home today, after all these years," Becky said. "The Rocking J has been on my mind constantly, ever since I was taken to Baltimore as a little girl."

Effie Sanderson seemed taken aback by her niece's statement. "I thought you were happy living with me in Baltimore," she sniffed.

"Dear Auntie," Becky said, pressing her aunt's hand consolingly, "of course I liked living with you, but you have to bear in mind that the Rocking J is where I have my roots, and New Mexico is where I belong. I shall miss Baltimore, of course, but this is my real home. Please say you understand."

"I understand only that I devoted the last nine years of my life to seeing that you were properly brought up, and what thanks do I get? You hardly express any regrets at leaving Baltimore at all. It is as if you could not wait to return to this wilderness. It is beyond me why perfectly sane people are attracted to this country, when the East has so much more to offer."

Immediately shifting her attention to Billy, the older woman said, "Were you born in this country, Mr. Bayes, or did you come here on Horace Greeley's advice?"

"It was neither, ma'am. I came here from Kansas after my ma died. Fact is, I took a job as a mule whacker with an outfit out of Independence, Missouri, traveling the old Santa Fe trail. After I arrived here I decided I liked it, and stayed.

"I expect I would have starved to death had Mr. Sanderson's ramrod not talked him into taking me on as a hand. I owe both Mr. Sanderson and Josh Clemens a debt of gratitude for going out of their way to help a greenhorn kid learn about ranching. They didn't have to do it, ma'am. It's just the way of people out here to help folks out whenever they can. I didn't see too much of that where I came from."

"With all due respect, Mr. Bayes, your previous life must have been even worse than I imagined, if your present situation is an improvement on it."

"You can't imagine, ma'am."

"Please, Auntie," Becky interrupted, "you are making Mr. Bayes very uncomfortable with this line of talk. Can we please discuss something else?"

"I am certain Mr. Bayes took no offense, dear. I am only curious as to why a seemingly intelligent young man would choose to settle out here, that is all."

"It doesn't bother me, ma'am. I've never regretted my decision to settle out here. Fact is, I'm right proud to be a part of it all."

Anxious to cut it short with Effie Sanderson, Billy said, "Not meaning to rush you ladies, but we'd best get an early start if we intend to arrive at the ranch before dark."

Traveling again in open country, Billy was happy to be on the final leg of his tiresome journey. It was a beautiful spring day and he marveled at the wildflowers that grew profusely on the surrounding hills, their many colors in sharp contrast to the washed-out drabness of the distant peaks and protruding rocks. Overhead, the sky was a clear, deep blue, with an occasional cotton-ball cloud hanging in suspension. More contented than he could remember, he breathed deeply of the perfume-laden air, giving thanks to an unknown god that he was who he was at this particular time and place.

Since the incidents with the Mexican bandits and the outlaws, Billy felt his luck had finally changed for the better. The trip back to the ranch was going as well as could be expected, and he was in love with the most beautiful girl in the whole world. At this point, he imagined, absolutely nothing could go wrong which could sour his disposition.

If only Effie Sanderson would now climb down off her high horse and be more understanding where he and Becky were concerned, everything in his world would be close to perfect. He did not really dislike the woman, and he could actually understand her concern for her niece, but the thing that really got his dander up about the older woman was her inflexibility in matters of the heart.

It was possible that she herself had never known true love, she being a spinster. If that were the case, how could she possibly be in sympathy with those who were in love? Such were Billy's thoughts when it all began to come apart.

First there was a sharp cracking noise, followed almost immediately by the piercing scream of Effie Sanderson. Billy wheeled the chestnut about, just in time to see the luggage slide onto the rutted trail. He had no doubt what had occurred; he had feared it might happen from the very moment when he overloaded the buckboard with all that luggage. An axle had sheared, dropping a rear wheel.

There followed a moment of stunned silence as the three travelers collected themselves and realized their situation, and although the broken axle presented to them an unexpected inconvenience, Billy was not unduly concerned by it.

They still had the horses, and Billy could see no problem in getting to the Rocking J before dark as originally planned. Still, he couldn't just leave the ladies' personal belongings scattered along the road, to be carted off by the first person who might happen along.

"What happened, Mr. Bayes?" Effie Sanderson said in her irritating, high-pitched voice. "I think something has broken."

"You're right about that, ma'am. Seems we sheared an axle. I've worried about that very thing happening all along. Wagon like this just wasn't meant to carry such a load."

"Well, can you repair it, Mr. Bayes?"

"There isn't a thing we can do about the wagon, ma'am. Someone from the Rocking J will have to bring out a spare axle and replace it later. There just isn't any other way."

"And just how do you intend to get word to the Rocking J, young man? I am not about to spend the night in this wilderness while you ride about the countryside for help," the older woman said, placing her hands on her hips for emphasis.

"We still have the horses, ma'am. You can ride a horse, I hope."

"What an absurd question. Of course I can ride. All Sandersons are expert horsemen—it is a part of our culture."

"Of course, ma'am. I meant no offense. If you and your niece could ride double on the bay, there's still time to make it to the ranch before dark."

"And just what do you propose to do about our luggage, young man? My entire wardrobe is in those trunks, not to mention my jewelry and other belongings. I will not just abandon everything on the road."

"No, ma'am, nor do I intend to. I'm thinking of carrying everything down the hill and hiding it behind an outcrop of rocks. There's a weatherproof tarp on the wagon to cover it—if that's suitable to you, that is."

"I suppose . . . if you think it will be safe until someone from the ranch can return for it."

"You just leave it to me, ma'am; I'll hide it well. In the meanwhile, if you have clothing suitable for riding, I would think about changing out of that dress."

While Becky assisted her aunt in digging through a trunk in search of her riding habit, Billy began to shoulder the remaining luggage down the hill, where he stored it carefully behind an outcrop. By the time he carried all the ladies' possessions to the hiding place and covered it with a tarpaulin, too much valuable time had elapsed to suit him.

"Ladies," Billy said, "we can save many miles of riding and much time if we leave the road and cut across the hills to the ranch, otherwise we're liable to find ourselves riding in the dark."

"Whatever you think, Mr. Bayes," Effie Sanderson said, agreeing with him for once. "It is your responsibility to lead us safely to the Rocking J, so I will trust to your judgement in the matter."

"Ma'am, I have only the one saddle, if you want it for the bay," Billy said to the older woman.

"A saddle is not necessary, Mr. Bayes. My niece and I both learned to ride bareback. Thank you, but you may keep your saddle."

Dragging the buckboard from the road, Billy then un-hitched the bay and removed the harness and shortened the reins for riding. Helping the ladies to mount the gentle horse, they were underway.

The party headed north through gently rolling hills and occasional rock spires that protruded from the barren ground like giant ghostly fingers. In the very far distance could be seen the small mountain range which marked the southern boundary of the Rocking J. Once over the mountains they would be on Sanderson property, and if all went well they could expect to reach the main house by late evening.

Ahead of them yet lay miles of dry, desolate country with little living vegetation, but Billy knew the location of several water holes along his planned route. He was in familiar country now, having ridden over most of it in the past four years in search of strays.

Taking their nooning at a spring surrounded by willows and cottonwoods, Billy watered the three horses and allowed them to graze while he joined the women in lunching on the cold food packed for them at the hotel dining room in Las Cumbres. Becky, judging from her movements, seemed no worse for wear after having ridden the bay horse bareback for the last couple of hours, but the movements of the older woman were exaggerated, telling him that she was making an attempt to hide the full extent of her punishment.

With no other motive in mind than to make the remainder of the trip easier on Effie Sanderson, Billy suggested to her that she ride the saddled chestnut, while he doubled on the bay with her niece.

For his attempt at chivalry, Billy received in return a five minute lecture from the indignant woman, pertaining to the impropriety of young men riding double with young ladies of breeding.

Throwing up his hands in resignation, Billy helped the older woman to remount the bay, while Becky made an animated face at him behind her aunt's back, all the while fighting to stifle her laughter.

Looking at the sun, Billy began to begrudge the time they had spent resting in the copse, even though he felt that the stop was necessary for the sake of the women and horses. But time was now their enemy.

The only way he could see them making it to the Rocking

J before dark was to ride straight through, making only those stops necessary to water themselves and the horses. Any delays other than that would put them behind schedule.

"How much farther, Mr. Bayes?" Effie Sanderson asked, and he could tell by the weariness in her voice that the strain of the ride was beginning to effect her.

"I'm still figuring about sundown, Ma'am—providing we don't meet with any delays on the trail."

"And what sort of delays are you speaking of, young man?"

"You know, those stops that don't fit into our plans. Take, for instance, that dark cloud building to the west of us. If it keeps heading this way, as I expect it will, we'll likely have to contend with some pretty rough weather before it's over. Hopefully, it'll blow itself out before it makes it this far, but out here a person can't be too certain of anything."

"Well, I certainly hope it blows itself out, Mr. Bayes. If there is any one thing that frightens me, it is the thunder and lightning that accompanies a storm."

"We'll just have to wait and see, ma'am."

Nervously, Billy watched the dark cloud building and blowing closer, and he was now certain they would not avoid it. Without alerting the ladies he began to scan the nearby cliffs, hoping for a ready shelter when the storm reached them.

Then, as the first splatters of rain began to pelt them, he spotted a large overhanging rock on the cliffs ahead. Although it didn't appear to be large enough to shelter the horses, he figured that the three of them could fit underneath it comfortably.

Leading the way off the trail, Billy spurred the chestnut and motioned for the women to follow him up the incline.

When his horse could not safely climb any higher, he quickly dismounted and tied him to a scraggly bush, leaving the Arabian's lead rope attached to the saddle horn.

The overburdened bay could only make it part way up the slope before he was played out, and Billy rushed down to assist the women in dismounting. Before he could secure the horse's reins, a clap of thunder caused him to bolt back down the incline, and Billy decided against chasing after him until after the storm had passed over.

Little good did it do them to take cover under the overhang; the gale-force winds drove sheets of water through the open sides of the rock and drenched them as though they had no cover at all. They crawled even farther beneath the ledge, burrowing like animals into the small space where the jutting rock protruded from the inclined cliff. And there they huddled miserably while the storm raged around them, seemingly without cease.

A heavy cloud covered the entire sky, from horizon to horizon, blanking out the sun and giving them the illusion of night. Continually, lightning flashed and thunder rolled, while rain fell in torrents, whipped by a wind that sought out every nook and cranny beneath the ledge where the already drenched travelers lay cringing against the seemingly endless onslaught.

In their immediate vicinity came an ear-splitting crack, accompanied by a blinding flash that caused the ladies to cry out in fear. The odor of ozone drifted up the incline and hung heavy in the air beneath the ledge.

Neither of the frightened women resisted as Billy reached out with comforting arms and pulled them tightly against himself. He could feel the convulsive shudders that racked the older woman's body, and he was concerned for her; having earlier admitted to being terribly frightened of thunder and lightning, Effie Sanderson must be in a state of near-panic by now, Billy felt.

But only moments after the bolt of lightning hit, the rain began to subside, followed by a clearing in the west. Soon, the sound of thunder was muffled by the distant hills to the east of them, as the fast-moving storm made its way out of the valley.

Thinking of the safety of the horses for the first time, Billy removed his protective arms from around the shivering women and walked out on the edge of the overhang and looked down the incline to where the horses were tied.

What he saw was not good. His chestnut lay lifeless on the ground, the rope securing the frightened Arabian still attached to the saddle horn.

Devastated, Billy ran down the incline and made a closer inspection of the chestnut. He was barely breathing, and it was obvious he had been struck by lightning; the entire length of one hind leg had been split open to the bone, and that was just the damage he could see. It was hard to tell just what his internal injuries were, if any.

But the horse didn't give up that easily, and made several feeble attempts to raise his head when Billy rubbed his neck. "I'm really sorry, old fellow," he said, choking his words. "You've been a good and faithful horse, and I've never ridden one better, but you're hurt bad and I have to end your suffering. I sure hope you can understand what I have to do."

Sadly removing his .44, Billy pointed it at the chestnut's head and closed his eyes as he squeezed the trigger. And as the echo of the shot resounded in the closed area, he wiped moisture from his eyes and turned to inspect the nervous Arabian.

The stallion, although pulling frantically at the lead rope

in fright, had suffered no visible physical damage from the lightning that hit the chestnut. Billy rubbed his neck and talked to him soothingly until he calmed down to where he no longer tugged at his restraint.

Removing the wet saddle from the chestnut, Billy carried it up the hill and placed it under the ledge until such time as he could return for it.

Becky, who had been watching the scene below, came over to Billy and placed her hand on his arm tenderly and said, "Oh, Billy, I am so sorry. I know how you loved that horse, and I know you're going to miss him. If there's anything I can do . . . "

"Thanks, Becky. A cowboy develops a relationship with his horse that few outsiders understand, but he wasn't the first horse I lost and probably won't be the last. I'll get me another in a couple of days."

Effie Sanderson, who was just crawling out of her burrow, attempted to straighten her wet, unkempt hair as she joined the two. "What was that gunshot I heard?" she asked.

"Billy's chestnut was struck by lightning and he had to shoot him," Becky said almost reverently.

"Oh, dear me. I am terribly sorry about your loss, Mr. Bayes, but whatever are we going to do now? How shall we ever get to the ranch on two horses?"

"Fact is, ma'am, we have no horses at all. The Arabian isn't broken for riding, and the bay ran off when you dismounted. He's probably running still."

"The Arabian! Is the Arabian unharmed?" Effie Sanderson asked.

"Seems to be, ma'am. I couldn't see anything wrong with him. He was a little frightened by the storm, but not much more than that."

"Thank heavens for that, at least. I would hate to see

anything happen to that horse after coming this far. It would simply devastate my brother.''

''Ma'am . . . Becky, I don't suppose I have to tell you ladies our situation. On the surface it doesn't look too good, I know, not having horses and all, but trust me and do as I suggest and we'll come out of it just fine. It's really not as bad as it appears.''

Effie Sanderson looked at Billy incredulously and studied his words before speaking. ''How can you say it is not as bad as it appears, Mr. Bayes? We are miles out in the wilderness without horses or food, and everyone is soaked to the skin and in danger of coming down with pneumonia. The situation certainly appears bad to me.''

''As I said, you've got to trust me, ma'am. This can be mighty rough country to survive if you try to go against it, and I've pretty much learned how to get by with the resources at hand. I won't tell you it'll be easy, but we'll make it.''

''Oh, this is just awful,'' Effie Sanderson whined. ''Whatever possessed me to leave the comforts of Baltimore and come to this forsaken wilderness.''

''Please, Auntie, you're not making our situation any easier by complaining. We're here and we'll have to make the best of it.''

''Yes, I know, dear, but I am soaked clear through, and I am cold and miserable,'' she cried. ''Why, I feel like a savage.''

The women, their clothes wet and caked with mud, and their hair hanging limply across their faces and down their backs, reminded Billy of a couple of bedraggled children, and had their predicament not been so serious he would have broken out laughing at the sight of them standing there beneath the ledge.

The first order of business, Billy knew, was to get a fire going, so that they could dry themselves. But he also knew it was going to be difficult to collect much dry wood after the soaker that had just passed through the valley.

Going down the incline to the valley floor, Billy began gathering deadwood from the sparse low-growing shrubs and bushes. Although wet on the surface, the twigs appeared relatively dry inside, and would burn well once started.

Having saved the old newspaper that still contained a little leftover food from the hotel in Las Cumbres, Billy removed it from his warbag and used it to start some twigs burning, lighting it with sulphur matches he carried in a waterproof tin. Gradually he added wood until he had a roaring fire beneath the overhanging rock.

Leaving the women huddled around the fire, Billy again headed for the valley floor to gather wood. Knowing that the small limbs and twigs would burn quickly once dried by the heat, he reconciled himself to the fact that he would have to make repeated trips down the incline to gather enough fuel to last them throughout the cool night.

Once he was satisfied that he had sufficient wood to last them, Billy rummaged through his warbag and inventoried the little food he carried. He grimaced at the sight of the rancid bacon, the partial bag of coffee and the uneaten tortillas from the hotel. This definitely would not feed them, he knew, as they had a long walk yet in front of them and they would need food for energy.

It was getting too close to the end of the day for Billy to scout the area for wild game, and he knew their situation was too critical to trust to luck alone if they were meant to survive their upcoming ordeal on foot. He made a decision he didn't particularly relish, but it was a thing that had to be done, and it had to be his secret alone.

Just at twilight, while the women were busy drying out the wet saddle blanket and bedroll next to the fire, Billy took his rifle and headed down the incline to the valley floor, leaving the ladies with the impression that he was going in search of wild game. But his action of taking up the rifle was only a ruse to later allay their suspicions when he returned to the ledge with fresh meat.

Although he had some slight misgivings about eating the flesh of the horse that had been like a friend to him, Billy discounted his feelings for the animal in favor of survival. Once out of sight in the valley, he fired the rifle into the air and waited behind the rocks until darkness descended.

Making his way back up the incline, Billy took out his hunting knife and removed a good part of the chestnut's hide from the exposed flank. Then, cutting out a large steak, he wrapped the still warm meat in the hide and started back to the campfire.

Returning to the ledge with his ''kill,'' Billy cut the meat into strips and hung it next to the campfire on sticks, letting it slowly dry as it cooked. A part of the dried meat would be eaten on the trail the following day, when they would not have the time to build a fire.

Chapter 13

It was Becky who first commented on the meat that was drying around the fire. "My, that certainly smells delicious. Is it elk?"

"Uh . . . no, antelope."

"It smells good all the same. I'm about famished."

"You intend to eat the flesh of a wild beast?" Effie Sanderson whined. "If you do not mind, I think that I shall wait until we get to the ranch before eating."

"Suit yourself, ma'am, but I strongly advise you to eat. We've a hard day yet in front of us, and you'll need food for energy."

Once the meat was done, Billy seasoned it with salt from his warbag, then took the coffeepot from the fire. "I have only the one cup, so we will have to take turns with it," he said, offering it to the older woman.

Billy and the girl ate ravenously of the meat, and when Effie Sanderson could take it no longer she said, almost shyly, "I think perhaps I shall try and eat just a bite, Mr. Bayes. As you previously stated, I shall need my energy."

"Just grab a piece and dig in, ma'am, that's what it's for."

Wolfing the meat down, Effie Sanderson said, "I could have been wrong about wild flesh, Mr. Bayes. That really was quite delicious. I shall try just one more piece—for my energy, you understand."

"Glad you like it, ma'am. There's plenty more where that came from." After the woman had developed a taste for it, Billy had fears that she would attack the meat he had dried for the next day's meals. But she was finally sated and leaned back contentedly.

"I suppose I owe you an apology, Mr. Bayes. That antelope was not at all bad, and certainly not what I expected of wild flesh."

Billy added twigs to the fire, unrolled the piece of horsehide and began cutting out crude moccasins for walking. The boots they all wore were designed for riding, and were not suitable for the kind of walking that lay in front of them. Working with his hunting knife and using strings of leather from his saddle, he began to fashion foot coverings sufficient for the walk to the Rocking J.

Finished, he handed each of the ladies a pair of moccasins, and naturally it was Effie Sanderson who voiced a negative opinion about the improvised footwear. "What is this, Mr. Bayes? You mean I am now to dress like a savage? Well, I shan't wear them. I may find myself reduced to sleeping on the ground and eating wild beasts, but I draw the line at dressing like an Indian."

"Ma'am, I advise you to reconsider and wear them. You won't walk very far in those fancy English riding boots."

"I shall take my chances, young man. You do as you choose, but I intend to maintain my dignity—even in this wilderness."

Billy shook his head and added more wood to the fire. Taking up a horse blanket he bid the ladies good night and started down the incline to where he had earlier removed the Arabian to a grassy spot on the valley floor.

The horse was becoming attached to him now, and whinnied in recognition as he approached. He nuzzled Billy as he rubbed his neck and talked to soothe him. "You're mighty friendly tonight, fellow. I'll bet you miss the chestnut, don't you?"

Still talking to the horse, Billy leaned against him and began rubbing his shoulder. Having made an instant decision, he then grabbed a handful of mane and eased himself onto his back. "Well, just you looky here, old son. And Becky said it couldn't be done."

His moment of glory was short-lived, however, as the horse suddenly hunched and reared on his front legs, sending the surprised kid spread-eagle to the ground. "Well, it was just a thought," Billy laughed, rubbing his bruised hip. "But you best get used to the idea of me sitting up there, because I'll be doing it again. You paying attention, horse? I'll be doing it again one day."

Billy collapsed on the spread saddle blanket and pulled it tightly over himself against the approaching cold. It had been a miserable day, he thought, and the night wasn't going to be a picnic either. And tomorrow? He would worry about that one at first light.

He wondered whether Paul Sanderson would send men looking for them after they did not arrive at the Rocking J as scheduled. Knowing the man as he did, he was most likely pacing the floor about now, realizing something had happened to them en route to the ranch. And if a search party was sent looking for them, they would have to come across the disabled buckboard and figure they took off through the hills.

He could just sit tight with the ladies at this location and hope searchers would ride in on them, but that would be taking a chance, as the rain had wiped out all traces of their tracks, and he was not at all certain that the searchers would even come in their direction.

The best plan, as he could see it, was to keep moving toward the Rocking J, as if there were nobody looking for them. That way, at least, they had a chance of eventually reaching their destination.

Wide awake and cold before first light, Billy led the Arabian to a recess in the rocks and let him drink of standing rain water, then he tied him to a good-sized shrub and climbed up the incline to where the women lay sleeping.

Throwing a handful of sticks on the still-warm coals, he placed the coffee pot over the fire and sat watching it boil. Awakened by his stirring about, Becky joined him at the fire and gave him a lazy hug.

Gosh, she looked good in the morning, Billy thought. He had first noticed the fact that morning in the outlaws' camp, and this morning was no exception. It was going to be a pleasure waking up to this girl for the rest of his life.

"It must have been rough sleeping out there with only one blanket," Becky said, brushing hair from his eyes.

"Oh, I'm used to it. Did you ladies sleep well?"

"As well as could be expected under the circumstances. Auntie complained something awful, but that's Auntie for you."

"Her complaining doesn't bother me now," Billy said. "After all, she's not accustomed to roughing it, being from back East and all. I'm only sorry she's been put through all this. And what about yourself? I haven't heard you complain even once."

"I can take it, Billy. This is where I'm from, don't forget. Me, I come from a long line of survivors. We didn't always have it so good at the Rocking J, you know. Why," she said, lowering her voice to a near whisper, "I even recall a time or two when we were reduced to eating horseflesh."

Billy felt the embarrassed flush. "You knew?"

"Well, I suspected. You see, what really convinced me was the Rocking J brand on the bottom of my new moccasins. I didn't think my father had gone to putting his brand on antelope. I kept it to myself because I knew you were only trying to do the right thing. But keep it from my aunt, for goodness sakes. She would never forgive you if she knew she had eaten your chestnut."

"What are you two laughing about so early in the morning?" Effie Sanderson said, raising herself on one elbow. "I cannot imagine anything that could be so humorous in this wilderness."

"Oh, nothing. We are only *horsing* around," Becky said, getting an elbow and a warning look from Billy.

"As I drifted off to sleep last night, I was hoping that all this was just a bad dream, and I would awaken this morning and find it so, but I can see that it is not a dream after all," the older woman said.

"As soon as you ladies have your coffee and make yourselves ready we'll be on our way," Billy told them. "We can make it to the ranch tonight if we don't have any more unforeseen problems—even on foot. The ranch is just over the mountains, you know."

"What problems could we anticipate?" Becky asked.

"Sore feet, for one thing," he answered, looking down at Effie Sanderson's bench-made riding boots in disgust.

In the pre-dawn hours, Josh roused half a dozen selected hands from their sleep and had them eat an early breakfast and prepare their horses and gear in preparation for the search for Billy and the Sanderson ladies.

The day before, many of the Rocking J hands had been taken off their regularly assigned duties and given the task of sprucing up the ranch in anticipation of the scheduled arrival of Paul Sanderson's daughter and sister. But in the late afternoon, a wide-ranging spring storm had ripped through the area, leaving swollen creeks and drowned Rocking J stock in its wake, and the hands had to work late into the night repairing damaged fences and rounding up scattered stock.

When Billy and his party did not arrive at the Rocking J as scheduled, Paul Sanderson was not unduly concerned. After all, it was a two-day trip from Bent Rock to the ranch, and any small delay in getting underway from either Bent Rock or Las Cumbres could cause a variation in their prearranged schedule. After discussing the situation with his ramrod, Sanderson decided to give the trio until the next evening before sending out a search party.

But later that evening there was a change in Sanderson's plans, when the bay showed up at the ranch without the buckboard. The only thing he and his ramrod could figure was that Billy and the ladies were caught in the open when the storm came through, and for some reason the bay was either cut loose from the buckboard, or else he had freed himself while being tethered.

At any rate, Sanderson was beside himself with worry. For the bay to show up at the ranch alone meant that something had gone wrong on the trail, and the uncertainty of the situation was the worst part of all for the concerned ranch owner. If he only knew what had befallen them he could take immediate steps to do something about it, but all he could do without information was send out the search party and hope for the best.

By first light Josh and his search crew were on the same trail that Billy was scheduled to travel between Las Cumbres and the ranch, and every man was reminded by the ramrod to keep his eyes peeled for anything either on or off the rutted trail that might offer a clue to the whereabouts of Billy and the ladies. Like Sanderson, Josh was uneasy not knowing what he could expect when he finally found the missing travelers.

Josh hoped nothing serious had befallen the kid which he could not handle on his own. Although he had a lot of faith in the abilities of the young hand, and had expressed as much to the ranch owner, Billy could have inadvertently made a costly mistake in his judgment somewhere along the line. But if he had, old Josh knew he could forgive him.

By the very fact that the bay had shown up at the ranch, Josh concluded, the horse had to have been in the vicinity when he found himself free. And it was for that reason they brought no extra mounts with them except for three saddled extras in case Billy and the ladies happened to be on foot when they finally found them.

But not knowing how far their search would take them, Josh gave orders to his men to pace their horses as much as possible. For even if it turned out that the missing three were in the near vicinity, their search could be more encompassing than planned, and it could take many miles of circling just to get a lead on their whereabouts.

Josh was hoping, though, that he and Paul Sanderson were worried over nothing. So what if the bay did come wandering up to the ranch alone? That didn't necessarily mean that Billy and his charges were in serious trouble. Why, it was possible they would come upon the three at any moment, walking the road to the ranch.

Brogen sat on a boulder next to the campfire as the half-breed applied a smelly concoction to the healing wound on his head. Whatever herbs were mixed with the mud the renegade had daily applied to his scalp, it was doing a good job, he had to admit, even if men and horses did give him a wide berth because of the offensive odor it exuded.

Although the laceration to his scalp no longer festered, he nevertheless felt a little dizzy at times, and the breed told him that he had probably sustained a concussion, which would likely heal on its own in a couple of more days.

Lupe, the breed who had taken him in a few days previously, was an ally of long standing. In his later outlaw years, when robbing banks and trains had become too risky a venture for Brogen and his remaining gang, they had combined forces with Lupe to rustle cattle together, taking from the ranchers just enough strays to make themselves a nuisance, but never getting so greedy at any one time as to cause a posse to come down on their lucrative operation.

There had always existed between the two gang leaders a good relationship, each assisting the other in times of need. Once, many years back, Brogen had provided the half-breed renegade a similar medical service by removing a bullet from his stomach and nursing him back to his feet. It had been touch and go whether the seriously wounded Lupe would survive at all, but Brogen had given him the same care and attention he would have given a member of his own family, and Lupe was not one to forget who his friends were.

The renegade's permanent camp could not have been more centrally located for his purpose of collecting strays. Situated in the high country near the Sangre de Cristos, it was the southern boundary which separated the sprawling Rocking J, owned by Paul Sanderson, and the equally huge Dobie Girl spread, owned by an absentee Englishman.

Lupe, whose very shrewdness accounted for the fact that he had thus far managed to run a successful rustling operation in the area without bringing retribution on himself, believed in keeping a low profile, never having more than a few renegade Kiowas in his camp at any one time. It was only when his cattle holdings became too large for his gang to drive to market by themselves that he recruited temporary help from other outlaw gangs hiding out in the nearby mountains.

The campsite itself had been well chosen; a hidden grassy valley in the higher elevations that commanded a view of the entire area for miles around, it contained within its walls an endless supply of water, as well as summer grazing for upward of a hundred head of cattle.

The camp had only one entrance, and from a point that afforded the rustlers a panoramic view of all the accessible approaches. The men in Lupe's gang stood lookout in rotating shifts, giving them the advantage of clearing out before a mounted posse could discover the hideout and bottle them in.

How Brogen had managed to make it to Lupe's camp in his previous condition was almost a miracle in itself, he figured. After having been struck in the head that night by Sanderson's hired hand and left for dead, he had regained consciousness sometime during the night and was barely able to crawl to his horse and ride out.

Several times on the trail Brogen had lost consciousness and fallen from his horse, only to later come to and remount and continue on his way to the camp of his old friend, where he knew he would be given a safe place in which to recuperate.

Possessed of will power and a strong sense of survival common to men of his breed, Brogen was not one to lie down and die without putting up a fight. And if there was any one thing that drove him, it was his thought of revenge on the kid who had practically come from out of nowhere and single-handedly did to his gang what lawmen and bounty hunters had been unable to do to to them for the last twenty years.

"How are you feeling today, my friend? Do you still have the dizziness?" The renegade studied the healing laceration on Brogen's scalp and nodded his head approvingly.

"Very little, Lupe—only when I raise myself too fast. Dang if I don't think I'll make it now, no thanks to that snot-nosed kid what laid me out."

"He works for the Rocking J you say? And he was with Paul Sanderson's daughter? I find that very puzzling about the daughter. For many years I have taken cattle from the Rocking J, and I have not seen this girl. I wonder how this can be, that Sanderson has a daughter I know nothing of?"

"She had just arrived from back East, she told Fisk and me. Something about living with an aunt in Boston—or Baltimore—I disremember exactly where. Now she's a purty little thing, I must admit, but she's crafty, and if I ever get my hands on her . . . "

The half-breed studied his words for a moment and laughed. "Unless I miss my guess, she had something to do with the wound to your head?"

"She had everything to do with it, the vixen. But she can't hole up in that big ranch house forever. One of these days she'll have to ride out, and when she does she'll pay."

"Revenge can sometimes be a sweet thing, but it can also cause a man to lose all reason and have it backfire on him. I have known many brave men who have entered the spirit world before their time because of their taste for revenge. As a friend I would advise you to reconsider this bitterness you have for the girl and maybe you will yet live to become an old man."

"I appreciate your concern, Lupe, but this is a personal

thing between me and her, and it's one of those things a man has to do.''

"How did you allow this—to let a boy crush your head with a rock? The Brogen I know is too smart for this.''

"I was stupid, that's how. I let some fine-looking female poison my thinking, and I dropped my guard.''

"Aha. Now I understand all. The bullet you once removed from my stomach was also because of a beautiful girl. I am still too embarrassed to talk about it—even to a friend.''

"So, how has it been with you, Lupe? I see you're still using a running iron,'' Brogen said, waving his hand at the small herd grazing below them.

"The same as always. We take a few from the Rocking J, a few from the Dobie Girl, a few here, and a few there. It adds up. But we still take only those few that stray past the mountain. And because of the storm that blew through yesterday we are overstocked, and must move them out very quickly before the grazing here is gone.''

"I guess you'll need somebody to watch your camp whilst you're gone, won't you? I ain't got a place to go for the time being, what with my partners dead and my hideout exposed. Fact is, I want to be close by to keep my eyes out for a certain kid and his girlfriend.''

"My home is your home, my friend. I only ask that you will do nothing that will bring a posse to my camp. Many years I have worked this area, and never have I given anyone reason to suspect I have a permanent hideout located on this mountain.''

"You don't have to worry about that, Lupe. I only need a temporary place to heal up, then I'll be riding out to the Rocking J range for a spell. Once I do what I aim to do there I'll be heading north. You don't have to worry about me leaving a trail.''

Chapter 14

It was later in the morning when Josh and his crew rode up on the crippled buckboard, and it was immediately apparent to the ramrod what had happened to delay Billy and the Sanderson women.

The storm of the day before having wiped out all signs, Josh found it impossible to ascertain the exact direction Billy and the ladies had taken after leaving the wagon, but knowing the kid as he did, it would have to be across country to the southern boundary of the Rocking J.

Yet several pieces of the puzzle were still missing. Where was the luggage, for instance? Surely they weren't packing it all, particularly considering the obvious fact they were shy the bay horse. And just why did the bay come wandering back to the ranch without them? What had happened out here to cause Billy to lose a horse he needed for getting his party to the Rocking J?

These were only several of the questions that went through the ramrod's mind as he studied the disabled buckboard. He decided to attack the puzzle in steps, beginning with the luggage. If it had been hidden in the area, he would find it.

"All right boys, I want everybody to fan out and circle the buckboard. We're looking for the ladies' luggage—and anything else we can find. Now, let's go."

It was only moments later when one of the hands discovered the camouflaged trunks and valises hidden between the rocks and covered with the waterproof tarpaulin.

"Good boy, Billy," Josh said under his breath. This was going to be easier than he had first thought. He was reading the kid like a book.

Picking two hands from his crew, Josh dispatched them to the Rocking J to bring back a spare axle and put the buckboard on the road with the luggage. Now came the hard part, tracking Billy without signs.

There was only one obvious route leaving the trail at that point that Billy could have taken, and Josh knew that. Later, farther along, his choices of routes would be several, but maybe by then they would find signs that had not been obliterated by the rainstorm. Signaling to his remaining four hands, Josh rode out into the wastelands.

It was a couple of hours later when they came to the copse and dismounted to water the horses. And while his crew rested their mounts, Josh began to poke around beneath the trees and bushes that bordered the water hole, looking for any sign that indicated Billy and his party had previously rested there. With the toe of his boot he pushed aside the tall grass and weeds that grew in abundance around the water, and he finally found what he was looking for.

There in the grass, barely visible except upon close inspection, were several beef ribs, the meat not eaten quite to the bone. Another piece of the puzzle fell into place. They had come through this way before the rainstorm, and they had food and water. Finding the food scraps gave Josh some relief from his concerns for the safety of Billy and his charges. Up to this point they did not appear to be in trouble. And on the other hand, there was the matter of the bay horse. . . .

No sooner had Josh put his men back on the trail and

crested the first rise when he saw the vultures circling in the distance. Icy fingers clutched at his heart, and a sense of foreboding instantly clouded his thoughts. Would this be where it all ended for Billy and the Sanderson women? Did they encounter a situation here that had got them all killed?

Shake it off, Josh, he told himself, you're much too old and experienced to be jumping the gun before you've seen the facts. Pointing at the vultures for the benefit of the men who were following him, he spurred his already tired mount up the trail.

Shortly, Josh and his men reached the source that had attracted the vultures. Scattering the carrion-eaters with a single shot from his .44, he began a close inspection of the chestnut's carcass. Although severely mutilated by the hungry vultures, he was still able to determine the animal had been struck by lightning, and that Billy—or someone—had finished him off with a gunshot to the head.

And the fact that a good portion of the hide had been removed from the chestnut with a sharp knife, along with a sizable steak, told the shrewd ramrod that it showed a good presence of mind on Billy's part, and that they were still eating. And if the missing piece of hide was any indication, he had fashioned moccasins for walking. Josh was impressed.

After the hands gathered around the ramrod and compared signs found in the area, it was determined that Billy and the women had left their camp just this morning, on foot, and they were leading a horse—most likely the Arabian, judging by the small hooves—and they had left a visible trail by which to track them.

All things considered, Josh felt better than he had felt since last night, when Billy and his charges failed to show up at the ranch as scheduled. From all signs, the kid was doing just fine, and all his problems were the results of a broken wagon and the unpredictable forces of nature.

A couple of miles from their starting point, as Billy knew it must eventually come, Effie Sanderson began to lag behind, and from the pained expression on her face he knew that her footwear was the problem. Over her protestations, he sat her on a nearby boulder and removed the undersized boots. Looking at the condition of her feet, he wondered how she had managed to walk this far without complaining about her obvious pain.

But to Billy, the fact remained that they were in serious trouble; the woman's feet were solid blisters, most having already burst, and it was very obvious that she could walk no farther.

Billy was in a quandary; he could either leave the woman alone while he continued on to the ranch to obtain horses, or else he could carry the slight-built woman piggyback and hope his strength didn't play out on him before they reached their destination. His greatest hope was that they would make contact with a hand from either the Rocking J or the Dobie Girl out searching for strays as they sometimes did after a severe storm.

His decision made, although reluctantly, Billy hung his warbag on the limb of a nearby cedar tree, then hoisted the mildly protesting Effie Sanderson onto his back and instructed Becky to take his rifle and the Arabian's lead rope and follow.

For a good half hour Billy walked the rock-strewn game path that meandered along the base of the mountain that was the south border of the Rocking J, occasionally grimacing in pain when a sharp-pointed rock found a tender part of his feet through his thin moccasins.

Finally, when the additional weight on his feet was more than he could stand, Billy stopped in the shade of a projecting rock and eased the woman to her feet and instructed her to sit on a nearby rock while he caught his breath.

"Mr. Bayes," Effie Sanderson said unconvincingly, "why not just leave me here while you go for help. I am too much a burden for you."

Supporting the weight of his upper body with his hands clenched just above the knees to catch his breath, Billy shook his head negatively and said, "Ma'am, we've come all this way together, and I'm not about to let you ladies or the Arabian out of my sight until I deposit you in the hands of your brother."

"Just look at yourself, Mr. Bayes, you can hardly catch your breath now, so how do you expect to carry me all the way to the ranch?"

"A step at the time if I have to, ma'am, but I'm not leaving you out here. As soon as we cut around this mountain, there's a good chance we'll run across one of the Rocking J hands out on the range—that's what I'm hoping, leastways."

Taking a deep breath, Billy again hoisted the woman onto his back and started up the trail, counting his steps to take his mind off the throbbing pain that was building in his legs. Another hour of walking, he figured, not counting rest stops, and they would come to a pass that would take them to the open range, where they stood a good chance of being spotted by one of the Rocking J hands as he headed in for the day.

Now straining under the weight of the woman, Billy was about to call another rest stop when out of the corner of his eyes he caught a glimpse of what appeared to him to be the tracks of an unshod horse. Curious, he lowered the woman to her feet and began following the tracks in the direction they had been walking.

Although the horse Billy was tracking was unshod, he could tell by the deep impressions of the tracks that it carried a rider, and that confused him. He never knew of anyone who rode around on unshod horses, except maybe an occasional Indian passing through, and very few of them traveled this part of the country anymore.

Shortly, Billy came upon a well-worn trail, where the rock and shale gave way to a bed of silt that appeared to have been deposited by the recent rainstorm. Everywhere were the fresh tracks of cattle, all heading up the mountain, and covering the cattle tracks were the hoofprints of at least five mounted horses, some shod and some barefoot.

Billy was more confused than ever by the signs, but he hastily concluded that perhaps hands from the Dobie Girl had been gathering strays which had been stampeded by the severe thunder and lightning that had accompanied yesterday's storm.

This was good news to Billy; he knew the cattle could not be driven over this particular part of the mountain, due to the sheer drop of the opposite side, so that likely meant they were being held temporarily in a box canyon at a higher elevation, until enough strays could be gathered to make a drive back to the open range.

With the tracks of the horses heading up the mountain, and none coming down, Billy took that as an indication he would be able to either borrow the horses he needed to get his party to the ranch, or else he could enlist help in getting horses from the Rocking J. Any way he looked at it, he could save everyone the torture of further walking.

Before following the tracks up the mountain, Billy figured, it would be best if he checked with the ladies and informed them of his intentions.

After giving the ladies the good news, Billy took his rifle, just in case, and started back up the game trail. Hardly had he turned the first bend when he was hailed by Becky, who was panting after him.

"Billy," she said breathlessly, "I only want to tell you to be very cautious. I can't explain it, but I have a bad feeling about you going up there. Call it a woman's intuition if you will, but something isn't quite right about it."

"Funny you should sense that; it doesn't feel right to me either, but I figure that's because I'm a little gun-shy lately, considering all I've been through with those outlaws."

"Just be careful," she said, kissing him quickly on the cheek and retracing her steps.

Following the many tracks up the mountain trail, Billy became even more confused as to why anyone would want to hold cattle at such a high elevation, particularly when there existed many good canyons below. He was still puzzling over this when the explosion sounded and the bullet splattered at his feet.

Billy immediately dove for cover, hitting the ground and rolling behind a large protective boulder. His own rifle at the ready, he peered around the rock and studied the high ground—but not for long. This time two shots were aimed at him, spraying his clothing with stone chips.

"Now this really gets my dander up," Billy said aloud. "Who in tarnation is shooting at me anyhow? I'm much too tired for this foolishness."

Well, he certainly had no time for games, and neither did he have the time to lay pinned behind a rock all afternoon. Whoever was shooting at him obviously meant business, and that being the case, it was doubtful they would be receptive to his request for horses.

Which brought him to the obvious conclusion that he had inadvertently walked into a nest of cattle rustlers. Everybody on the Rocking J had always known they were out here somewhere; just too many strays had come up missing over the years without an explanation.

At this point, Billy decided, he could do one of two things; he could either take the long way to the ranch, carrying Effie Sanderson on his aching back and avoiding the rustlers altogether, or else he could confront them head-on and take by force the horses he needed.

He decided on the latter plan, as he figured he could save valuable time by taking on the rustlers, inasmuch as he wasn't certain of the odds against him.

Billy knew he could neither go straight up the hill, nor back down the trail, because of the hidden gunman who had put him behind the rock. That fact left him with but one choice; he would have to take a chance and go to his left, jumping from rock to rock until he found safety behind a nearby concealing ledge.

But no serious action is taken without a plan; Josh had drilled that fact into him over the years. Taking his hat in his hand, Billy tossed it from behind the boulder, into a nearby bush, and immediately ran for the next protective rock.

He hated seeing the new hat sacrificed to the bullet that tore through its crown, but he could always buy a new hat. By the time the anonymous gunman realized he had been suckered, Billy was already behind the ledge and sprinting like a jackrabbit for higher ground, the rocks offering him total concealment.

As Billy made his way along the rim of the canyon, the

surprised Lupe gathered his force of four renegade braves and had them fan out along the entrance to his hideout. The half-breed had a difficult time in gathering his thoughts for a workable defensive plan; his entire strategy had been based on clearing off the mountain upon the early sighting of mounted men riding in from miles out.

Now, because of the fallibility of that plan they were trapped like hobbled horses, an easy target to the man who lurked somewhere above them.

As far as Lupe knew, they were only up against a single intruder who had managed to broach their defenses. But that meant nothing; the man could be an advance scout for a larger party who lay in hiding, awaiting his return, and if that was the case, they had to kill him before he could report back.

Calling out to a man who maintained a defensive position nearby, Lupe pointed to the upper rim of the canyon wall. Nodding his head in the affirmative, the brave placed his knife between his teeth and began the laborious task of ascending the sheer cliff.

Billy, who was unaware of his advantage over the superior forces below, actually felt himself to be the one at a disadvantage. With this thought in the back of his mind, he took pains to conceal his presence on the rim overlooking the rustlers' camp.

From his position, however, it slowly dawned on him that he could control the only entrance to the canyon, but the realization gave him little comfort. He was in a hurry to get his hands on several of their horses, not spend the entire afternoon preventing them from escaping.

If things were going to happen soon enough to please him, he would have to be the one to initiate it, he finally concluded. And because one of their bunch had tried to kill him earlier without warning, he felt completely justified in picking them off whenever they showed themselves. Having convinced himself of the morality of what he had to do, he fired a shot into the air to make his position known.

No sooner had the echo of his shot subsided when a half-naked warrior sprung from behind a rock to his left, wielding a raised knife. Reacting instantly, Billy rolled on his side from where he lay and brought his rifle butt against his attacker's face, hearing the crunch of bone and feeling the splatter of blood as the man crumpled on top of him.

Rolling the dying man off him, Billy put the canyon to his back and faced the direction in which the Indian had attacked him. Now things were moving, he felt.

Having exposed himself as he stood over the squirming man at his feet, Billy heard the bullet that went past his head. Falling quickly to the ground, he peered over the edge of the rim as another shot was fired at him from a group of rocks near the camp's entrance.

Aiming at the slightly exposed part of the man who had fired at him, Billy got an immediate reaction. Probably figuring to try for better concealment, the Indian, along with another who was sharing the rock, attempted to run for it, and Billy leveled them with two shots fired in rapid succession.

From where he and his lieutenant were hidden behind a tattered white duck tent near the corral, Lupe, seeing two of his best men gunned down by the man on the overlooking rim, became nervous. "We will wait and see if Santo can get to the rifleman above us," he said to the man lying beside him. "If not, we had better try to make a run for it. I do not wish to remain here and be picked off like an animal."

"Yes, Lupe, I think maybe you are right. At least a

coward lives to fight another day, I am thinking. But what of your friend—this Brogen. Will we not take him with us?''

"He is a survivor, that one. He has hidden himself with the cattle. I will not worry about him.''

"Wherever is Santo?'' the man said to Lupe. "If he has succeeded in surprising the intruder we should have known it by now.''

"He has been gone for a long time, so I think he is probably dead. Maybe it is time for us to leave this place.''

"Yes, Lupe, but it will be very dangerous to bridle the horses. How are we going to do so without being seen?''

"It is a risk we must take. We will stay very low until we are ready to ride out, then we will scatter the horses and try to confuse him.''

Crawling on their hands and knees, the two renegades made their way among the horses in the corral and used them as shields while they quickly bridled their own mounts.

From his perch above them, Billy reloaded his rifle and waited. He could see what the rustlers were up to in the corral and he also figured they would scatter the remaining horses in an attempt to throw him off, but he was having none of that. Training his rifle sights on a point where the defile narrowed, he waited.

Removing the rails from the corral, Lupe said, "I am ready, my friend. You say when.''

"Whenever you are ready, Lupe.''

"Then let us go—now!''

Billy figured for a moment to let the men escape, but thought better of it. The ladies and the Arabian were waiting for him down below, and it would be too easy for the renegades to take them as hostages before he could grab one of the horses and make it to them.

His first shot knocked a man from his mount, but the following round was low, downing the man's horse. Through the dust kicked up by the running horses, Billy saw the downed man swing his rifle toward him and begin firing wildly, peppering the ground around him. Taking careful aim, Billy fired off a round at the stationary man, causing him to drop his rifle and grab his chest with both hands. Eyeing Billy across the void for a moment, the renegade then dropped lifeless to the ground.

Billy was confused; so far he had dispatched five men, but he could count six horses below him. Either another man was lurking about the area, or else the rustlers kept a spare horse. And not knowing which, he decided to wait before descending onto the canyon floor.

Chapter 15

Josh thought he heard the muffled sound of distant rifle fire. Motioning for his party to stop, he listened for several minutes, but the sound did not resume. "Must be hearing things," he said to the nearest man to him, "but I swore I heard rifle shots."

"I didn't hear nothing, boss. Then, again, I can't hear much of anything over the noise of the horse's hooves on this infernal shale."

"Well, we'll move on, but try to keep your ears open for shooting. I ain't exactly certain yet I didn't hear something."

Farther down the game trail, Josh pulled his horse to an abrupt halt and studied his surroundings. Suddenly, for no apparent reason, the horse they had been tracking left the trail and his hoofprints were lost in the rocks. Could be Billy had decided to take a rest away from the trail, Josh figured. He was surprised he'd gone this far between rests.

They had figured early on that Billy was carrying one of the women on his back, because they had found the riding boots on the trail where they had been abandoned, and the absence of the third set of prints indicated as much.

Searching the area on foot, Josh and his men were able to track the Arabian by looking for overturned pebbles and scrape marks. Following the signs around a large boulder, they came face to face with the horse they had been tracking all day.

"Mercy, what a horse," said Hobbs, one of the older hands.

"You said it," Josh agreed. "If I had to take a guess, I'd say we found Sanderson's Arabian. But our job is only part done. What do you suppose became of the kid and those ladies?"

"Hey, boss," whispered one of the hands, "I just saw a movement in that crevice over yonder, like something flashed—a gun maybe."

"Let's check it out," Josh said. "Something mighty peculiar's going on here, and I aim to find out what."

Leading their horses, Josh and his men walked over to the crevice, only to be met by a six-gun in the hand of a frightened girl.

"Just you hold it right there. I know how to shoot this thing, and I don't mind doing it," she said nervously, waving the gun about.

"Whoa, now just you hold on there, missy. If you're Rebecca Sanderson, your pa sent me and the boys out looking for you when you didn't show up at the ranch. Name's Josh Clemens, and I'm the ramrod at the Rocking J."

"And me, miss. I'm Hobbs, and I taught you to sit a horse when you was just a biddy thing. Don't you remember old Hobbs?"

"Yes, of course I do," she said, lowering the gun. "Thank goodness you've shown up. I believe Billy's run into some trouble up ahead."

Leaving one man to stay with the women, Josh and his remaining hands mounted their tired horses and started them up the trail in the direction Billy had earlier headed.

And as Billy had before them, they came upon the many

cattle and horse tracks at the base of the well-worn trail leading up the mountain. Not taking the time to reason it out, they checked the loads in their guns and cautiously started up the incline.

Soon they heard the sound of rapid hoofbeats coming down the trail, and immediately Josh signaled his crew off to the side. They hid themselves behind a group of boulders and cleared their holsters. Whoever the horsemen were, they were primed to face them after they rounded the last turn in the trail.

Josh was both surprised and relieved when Billy burst into the open, riding bareback and leading two saddled ponies. Reining his horse out onto the trail, the ramrod removed his hat and held it in the air to flag the kid down, a wide grin on his face.

Reining his mount alongside Josh's, Billy merely said, "What took you so long, Boss?"

The still-grinning Josh studied Billy for a long minute before speaking. Satisfied with what he saw, he said, "Got yourself a new hat, I see."

"Yep. Bought it down in Bent Rock."

"Come with that bullet hole already in the crown?"

"Nope, fellow up the trail punctuated it for me, but I broke him of the habit."

"Tell me more about that fellow up the trail," Josh said.

"Well, there were five of them, actually."

"Were?"

"Yeah, well . . . they fired the first shot. All I wanted was to borrow a couple of horses."

"What else did you see up there, kid?"

"A box canyon with about fifty, sixty head of cattle with Rocking J and Dobie Girl brands on them."

"Probably accounts for those strays we couldn't find after

the storm," Josh said, turning serious. "And that pinto you're leading sure looks familiar. Reckon we'll find its owner up there, huh?"

"I can't say, boss, but I blew a fellow off him—a half-breed, he appeared to be."

"Sure sounds like Lupe all right. That breed's been slicker than bear grease. Been siphoning off strays in these parts for years, but nobody's ever come close to pinning him down before now."

"Look, boss, I hate to call this pow-wow short, but Sanderson's ladies are waiting for me down the trail, and I best get these horses to them and move them out."

"They're fine, kid. Old Hobbs is with them. You go ahead and join them and head out for the Rocking J, and me and the boys will check out that hill—maybe clean up the mess you made."

"Whatever you say, boss, but be careful, will you. Might not mean much, but those varmints had six horses up there and I only counted five bodies."

"If he's still up there and we happen to run across him, then he'd better be the one that's careful, that's all I can say."

Billy kicked his mount and started down the trail to where the others waited. He suddenly felt better than he'd felt in days. At last his long ordeal was over and he was back among friends.

Becky spurred her horse and left the waiting group when Billy rode into view. Even with her disarrayed hair and dirt-caked clothing, he thought, she was still the most beautiful girl in the world. And now that they were near their journey's end they could find time for socializing, without being chaperoned by her hawk-eyed aunt.

As she came alongside him, her smile gave way to shock.

"Billy," she said, backing away, "that horse you're riding—where did you get it?"

"Why, I took it from some rustlers up there. What's wrong?"

"That's the horse Brogen was riding the day I encountered those outlaws on the trail. I'd know that sorrel anywhere."

"Are you sure? Looks like an ordinary enough horse to me."

"I'm absolutely certain it's the same horse. I recognize it by the scar over its nose. That was the first thing I noticed when they blocked the trail that day."

"I can tell easy enough," Billy said, dismounting. "I ought to; I spent an entire day following his tracks."

It took only one quick look for Billy to confirm Becky's suspicions about the horse. But he wondered what it was doing in the rustlers' corral.

"My guess is," he said to Becky, "Brogen collapsed somewhere on the trail after he rode off that night, and these rustlers found his horse."

Billy hoped that was the case, leastways; in his haste to round up the horses he needed, he didn't take the time to check out the rustlers' camp as thoroughly as he should have. If Brogen was up there somewhere, chances were that Josh and his boys would flush him out.

Maybe he should ride back up the mountain and tell Josh about his suspicions. He'd already warned him of the possibly of a sixth man being in the camp. And knowing Josh as he did, Billy concluded that the old ramrod would approach the camp with caution.

"We're almost home, Becky, so let's forget about Brogen—and all that trouble we had out on the trail. Why, I'm so awfully glad to be getting back to the Rocking J that even mending fences is beginning to look good to this old boy.''

''Why, Billy Bayes, if I have any say in it, you'll not be mending fences or anything else for a few days. With all you've been through this past week you deserve a rest. Besides, I'll need someone to show me around the ranch.''

''That all sounds good to me, Rebecca Sanderson, but I work for Josh Clemens, and that old cowboy has a mind of his own where I'm concerned.''

''Oh yeah?'' Becky laughed. ''He works for my father, so we'll see about that.''

After Billy had removed the accumulated trail dust and changed into clean clothing, he walked over to the main house to return the excess of gold coins to the ranch owner.

Paul Sanderson himself met Billy at the kitchen door and led him to the barn where the Arabian was stalled.

Accepting the gold pouch, Sanderson absently put it in his pocket and said, ''Billy, I hate to say it, but I'm more than a little disappointed in your performance while accompanying my sister and daughter to the ranch. I sent you to Bent Rock on my ramrod's advice, with the simple task of getting them here safely. Because of your incompetence my sister is bedridden with her feet, and I've had to send to town for a doctor to attend her.''

''Sir, there are circumstances that you apparently aren't aware of. If I could just tell you about what happened—''

''That will not be necessary,'' Sanderson interrupted. ''I've had a long talk with my sister and she has told me all I need to know about your performance. According to her, you were irresponsible from the very moment when you showed up at the train depot in Bent Rock.

''For the most part, I've always left the hiring and firing

of the hands to the discretion of my ramrod, but in his absence I am telling you that you are no longer needed at the Rocking J. I'll fill Josh in on the facts when he returns from whatever tomfoolish chase you sent him on earlier in the afternoon.''

Taking a roll of bills from his pocket, he held them out to Billy. ''Here is your wages for the month, plus a month's severance. Inasmuch as I do not normally furnish a man with a horse when he is dismissed from my services, I will make an exception in your case. Up until this trip to Bent Rock, I have been completely satisfied with your work here at the Rocking J.''

It was all Billy could do to hold his temper in check. ''You can keep your money, Mr. Sanderson. If I've disappointed you, then I didn't earn it, and I couldn't in all conscience take it. The same goes for the horse you offered me. I have a mount I came by on the trail, and I don't think there's any claim on it.''

''No hard feeling then?'' Sanderson said, offering his hand.

Billy rejected the proffered hand and turned sharply in his tracks and headed for the bunkhouse to gather his possessions.

Tired, confused, and angry, Billy fought to keep his composure in front of the hands who gathered around his bunk to watch him pack his pitifully few belongings. They were sympathetic, all, for they knew him to be a dedicated, hardworking hand, and his past loyalty to Paul Sanderson was unquestionable in their minds. If it could happen to Billy Bayes, of all people, it could just as easily happen to any one of them, were their silent thoughts.

Without a word being spoken, Rollo, one of the older hands, removed his hat and placed a crumpled bill into it and passed it to the next man. And when the hat had made its round amongst the hands there, Rollo removed a wad of money and pressed it into Billy's hand.

To have refused the collection would have offended his friends of long standing, so Billy stuffed the money in his pocket and wordlessly shook each of their hands in turn, then he took his saddlebags and rifle and walked out into the night and mounted the waiting sorrel.

Entering the Golden Girl, Billy found an empty table in a far corner and ordered a bottle of whiskey, throwing the wad of crumpled bills on the table in front of him.

Nathaniel, the owner of the bar, personally delivered the bottle to Billy and said, "Now, Billy, the last time you came in here like you had a chip on your shoulder, you near ruint me. Would you like to pay off that account before you get plastered and create a new one—whilst you still have the money?"

"Just take what I owe you on account," Billy said, pushing the pile of bills toward him.

"This should do it," the man said, smoothing the bills in his hand.

"Tell me, Nat, do you ever drink? Funny, but as often as I've been in here I've never seen you down a shot."

"Sure, kid, I sometimes take a drink or two with those I consider a friend."

"Will you have one with me? I'll buy."

"Not this swill I pass off on you cowboys. I'll get us a bottle of the good stuff."

"Shows what I know," Billy said. "I thought all this time I was drinking the good stuff."

Nathaniel returned with a bottle of bonded whiskey and filled two glasses and made a toast. "Here's to good friends."

"My sentiments exactly. I'll drink to that."

Emptying his shot glass, the bar owner folded his arms and placed his elbows on the table, studied Billy for some moments, and said, "Okay, kid, what is it this time? Josh pushing you too hard again? The little Chamberlain girl won't give you the time of day, like the last time? Which is it?"

"Nat, you must get around. My guess is that every man who's ever been in this place has laid his problems on you at one time or the other—that's my guess."

"You could say that, kid. You got something on your mind?"

"Paul Sanderson just ran me off the Rocking J. It all happened so dang fast that my head is still swimming, and the thing is I didn't deserve it, and he wouldn't listen to my side of it."

"Dang, kid, that is tough. And you say he wouldn't discuss it with you? That doesn't sound like the Paul Sanderson I know. I've always known him to be a fair man, and what you just told me makes no sense at all."

"Oh, it wasn't like he didn't give me a reason. You see, it's this sister of his, she poisoned his mind against me. I was sent to escort his sister and daughter from Bent Rock to the Rocking J, and she gave him some cock and bull story about me not doing my job like I was supposed to have done."

"No, kid, that doesn't sound like Paul Sanderson at all, and I know him better than most hereabouts. Why, we were friends back when he was only running about sixty, seventy head of cattle on that place, and most of them being moss horns and scrubs he rounded up in the hills. It was me that staked him when his wife and kid were starving, and every-

body else in town thought he was a bad risk. Yeah, I reckon
me and him go back a-ways.''

"You don't have to convince me about Sanderson, Nat.
I've been on the Rocking J payroll for nigh on to four years
now, and I've never known the man to be less than fair
with all his hands. It's that contrary sister of his that set
him against me, I know it.''

"Kid, you have to be leaving something out of what you
just told me. It's a slow night and I got nothing better to
do but listen. Why don't you just start from the beginning
and tell me everything. Maybe together we can hit on a
solution to the problem you're having.''

Billy refilled his shot glass and began to relate his adventures, starting from the time when he returned to the
ranch after spending the winter in the isolated line shack.
He talked without interruption, omitting no detail of his
odyssey, and when he was finished he again refilled his
glass and looked at the captivated bar owner questioningly.

"What do you think, Nat?'' Billy said.

Nathaniel only studied Billy incredulously and shook his
head for several long minutes. Then he filled his shot glass,
downed it, cleared his throat, and said, "Billy, if any man
other than yourself had come in here and told me what you
just did, I'd say he had too much to drink, or else he was
just full of himself and was spinning yarns. But I know
you, and I also think you're capable of doing everything
you said you did. I can't figure why you were fired over it.
Heck, if anything, you deserve a raise for what you did for
Sanderson.

"Now, if you ask me—and I recollect you did—I'd say
that sister of his either left something out of her story, or

else she added something to it—something she dang well knew would put you in a bad light with her brother.''

"Thunderation, Nat, what was the very first thing I came in here telling you? Of course his sister lied to him about me. Why else would he give me my walking papers?''

"Now don't you go getting yourself all riled up, kid. Let's put our heads together and figure this thing out. Now, you say you have this thing for Sanderson's daughter, and her aunt is set against it. If I were a gambling man—and I sure as shootin' am—I'd say you have gone and fallen for the wrong little filly.

"Has it occurred to you that Sanderson's sister might have told him about your romantic interests in his little girl, and he might also be dead set against it? Have you even considered that possibility?''

"You know, Nat, you might just have a point there. It did cross my mind way back that Sanderson might be against me having a thing for his daughter. Could be why he ran me off without an explanation.''

"Kid, it sure sounds to me like the four of you should get together and talk this thing out. Why don't you have Josh Clemens set something up?''

"Nat, you just don't know what you're asking. I don't have much to my name but my guns and a pair of saddlebags, but I sure as heck got my pride. If things need talking about, let Sanderson be the one to find me. He had his chance to talk when he ran me off his place.''

"Look, kid, from what you told me, you've had a long day, and it shows. Why don't you take an empty room upstairs and get yourself some needed rest—my treat. Everything always looks better after a good night's rest.

Besides, if you hit that bottle much harder, this place might need another renovation job, and I don't think you can afford it.''

Billy didn't argue the point with Nathaniel about needing rest; it had been a long day, and he was beginning to feel the effects of it.

Chapter 16

It was before daylight when Billy opened his eyes and it was another few minutes before he was able to determine where he was. Nathaniel was wrong; it was the next day and things didn't look any better to him than they had the night before. The confusing thoughts that were swirling in his head when he finally fell off to sleep were still with him—nothing had changed.

"Come out of it, Billy," he said softly to himself. "Just who said life is easy anyhow. You can lie here all day and feel sorry for yourself, or you can get out of bed and make life happen. After all, you've survived much worse than this."

After his pep talk to himself, Billy jumped from bed and dressed. What he needed to clear his thoughts was a solitary ride into the hills. He most always seemed to think better when he was sitting the saddle. Maybe by the time he returned from his ride, the restaurant would be open for breakfast. All at once he was hungry.

The town was still sleeping when Billy let himself out and walked down the back stairs into the street. It was his favorite time of the day, and he looked forward to seeing the sunrise from the saddle.

Pulling the stable door open, Billy adjusted his eyes to the darkness inside. He was surprised that the stable man was not yet about, for it had been his experience that the old man was usually the first in town to awaken and he always had a lit lantern hanging from the rafters just inside the door. For some unknown reason, Billy felt a cold tingle in his neck and his hand slowly slid down to the butt of his six-gun.

"Just you take it out real easy like and throw it into that first stall there," came Brogen's unmistakable gravelly voice. "If you ain't real quick about it I'll blow your head off right where you stand."

Slowly, not having any choice, Billy removed his gun as ordered and tossed it into the empty stall in front of him. He now found himself at the total mercy of a man whom he had twice beaten at his own game, and whose vengeful drive now represented an imminent danger to him.

His only hope, as Billy could see it, was that the man would play with him for a while, in order to better fulfill his vengeful needs, and time, he felt, was on his side. If history had any bearing on Billy's seemingly hopeless situation, Brogen would eventually make a miscalculation, and when he did, he must be ready to take advantage of that mistake instantly.

"Bet you thought you would never see me again, huh? Shows what you know, kid. A real man would've finished me off with that rock. Now you're gonna pay for your mistake."

"Before you finish me off," Billy said, partly out of curiosity and partly to stall for time, "were you in that rustler's camp yesterday?"

"Went and hid amongst the cattle when the first shot was fired. I knowed there was no way out of that canyon. Pretty smart, huh?"

"I guess so," Billy said, patronizing him. "But how did you know to find me in town?"

"I didn't. I rode in last night on one of those ponies you left up there, and the first thing I see when I dropped him off here is my own horse. I inquired of him, and the old man told me who it was that stalled him here. So I just waited. Figured you'd be along directly."

Without a warning, Brogen brought his rifle butt down on Billy's right shoulder, knocking him to the floor.

Desperately seeking an advantage, Billy lay motionless where he fell, feigning unconsciousness, but Brogen, who was not fully convinced, poked him in the ribs with the barrel of the rifle and laughed.

Grimacing in pain, it was all Billy could do to keep from crying out and giving himself away. Now, thinking perhaps Billy was indeed knocked unconscious, Brogen again used the point of the rifle to nudge him in the ribs, only this time he made the error of probing too long, giving Billy the reaction time he needed to quickly reach out with both his hands and swing the rifle away from his body, while at the same time forcing the butt hard into the outlaw's groin.

Releasing his hold on the gun, Brogen yelped in pain and grabbed for his crotch, allowing the weapon to fall into the dirt and hay.

Now, seeing the opening he was looking for, Billy was instantly on his feet, landing a left-handed jab to the unguarded face of the big outlaw, but hardly doing the damage he had hoped. Frustrated by the unwillingness of the man to do little more than flinch under his best punch, he decided to change his tactic by diving for his legs in an attempt to throw him off balance.

But even that maneuver was only partly successful, in that Brogen grabbed Billy with his powerful hands and took him down with him. On impact with the ground, the outlaw was momentarily stunned, and released the kid just long enough to again allow him the time to fire off several rapid punches to his face.

Now, beginning to feel the brunt of Billy's charge, Brogen became a raging bull, simultaneously flailing his arms and rolling his body to dislodge his adversary.

Once more on his feet, Billy concentrated on Brogen's midsection, using his superior speed and agility to take advantage of weaknesses in the older man's guard and land quick blows to his stomach.

But the outlaw's big girth offered him insulation against the kid's fusillade, and before Billy realized what had happened, he found himself in a bear hug that nearly blanked his mind.

That the big outlaw was strong was belatedly apparent to Billy, as he struggled to find a purchase on his thick neck with his free right arm. But having been partially numbed and weakened by the earlier blow to his shoulder with the rifle, he hadn't the strength to follow through with his plan to dislodge himself from the man's encircling arms.

Feeling the air being forced from his lungs, and experiencing the early dizziness of a blackout, Billy was nearly paralyzed by the fear that he was slowly being squeezed to death, and in his failing consciousness he thought of the thick-bladed Green River knife hanging from his belt.

Too weakened to do more than prick at the layer of fat covering Brogen's waistline, Billy soon found it enough to cause the man to release his death hold and allow him the time to stumble out of harm's way long enough to fill his lungs with much-needed air.

Brogen, by now, found himself standing over his rifle, and slowly took it in his hands and aimed it at the kid. With a surge of adrenalin brought on by his strong sense of survival, Billy drew back the razor-sharp knife and threw it at the outlaw with all the strength he could muster.

With the hilt of the ten-inch knife protruding from Brogen's chest, his face registered complete surprise before he toppled backward onto a derelict surrey, sending it crashing beneath his weight. In his death throes, a single round from the rifle was fired into the ceiling.

Billy flung himself down on a nearby bale of hay and put his face in his hands and collected himself. It took several minutes for the full impact of what had just occurred in the barn to fully sink in.

Only in the sense that his own life was spared did Billy take satisfaction in seeing the outlaw lying lifeless on the cluttered stable floor. A peaceful person by his very nature, he had never pointed a gun at a man in anger until he encountered the Brogen gang, and already, in the past week, he had taken a total of eight lives, and in every case he felt he had been forced to kill in order to protect his own life.

Now that the last of the outlaws was dead, maybe there would be an end to the violence which had plagued him since it first began that night when he was forced to shoot Beak in self defense. Billy certainly hoped so, for he was growing sick of death and violence.

With drawn six-gun, Marshal Winfield McDuff entered the open door of the stable and looked over the scene. Recognizing Billy at once, he said, "Want to tell me what's going on, Billy?"

"That owlhoot over there is called Brogen," Billy said, gesturing with his thumb. "He jumped me when I came into the stable. He meant to kill me and we tussled a bit."

The marshal walked over to the man lying amid the broken wood and cobwebs and studied his face. "Yep, that's Brogen, sure as shooting. It's been a long time, but I recognize him yet, and according to my calculations the Brogen gang ceases to exist.''

"That's the way I figure it, marshal, but how did you know? The others got it down near Bent Rock—just recently.''

"You saved me a trip out to the Rocking J, Billy. I got a wire from the marshal over in Bent Rock just yesterday. Seems I'm to give you a draft on the local bank in the amount of $5,000, the outstanding reward money for those other two, Beak and Fisk.''

"That's an awful lot of money, marshal, and it couldn't come at a better time. You see, I no longer work for the Rocking J, and I can sure use the money to start my own spread.''

"What do you mean, you don't work for the Rocking J? You quit or something? You always said you were satisfied working there—leastwise I got that impression.''

"Well, it's a long story, marshal, but Sanderson gave me my walking papers last night.''

"Sanderson? I always thought Josh Clemens did the hiring and firing at the Rocking J. How does he feel about this?''

"I don't think he knew about it. He was up in the hills looking over that rustlers' camp when it all happened. Doubtless, he won't know about it until this morning.''

"Whoa, kid. Now just you back up to that part about a rustlers' camp.''

"Seems I walked in on that half-breed Lupe's hideout yesterday, and we had ourselves a confrontation. It came down to a shoot-out and they got the worst of it.''

"Kid, there seems to be some in-betweens missing here. Why don't we just mosey on up to my office and talk this thing over for the record. I *am* the marshal around here, and it would seem I'm entitled to know about these things when they happen in my jurisdiction.''

"Sure, marshal, it wasn't like I was intending to slight you. I just had too much on my mind.''

Pouring himself a cup of coffee from a chipped enamel pot, the marshal indicated several battered tin cups hanging from the wall. "Fresh pot, Billy. Help yourself.''

Throwing his feet on his spur-scarred desk, the marshal took a telegram from the clutter and flipped it to Billy. "The wire from the marshal up in Bent Rock," he offered. "I near swallowed my cud when I read where you bested that varmint Clay McGruder, alias Beak, in a shootout. You just don't know how many years I've been after that gent.

"And that fellow Fisk I don't know a lot about, but some rich shipping tycoon back East put up the reward for him. Bet you made a whole passel of bounty hunters unhappy, too. They been beating the bushes around here for years looking for that gang.

"Now, there's the matter of Brogen. Don't know yet what the reward is for him, but doubtless there is one. I'll have to make inquiries about that one and let you know.''

The marshal was interrupted by a young deputy, who walked into the office and nodded curtly at Billy before taking down one of the tin cups and pouring himself some coffee from the steaming pot.

"Before you make yourself too comfortable, Jenkins," the marshal said to him, "go rouse the undertaker out of bed and take him to the livery stable. Seems he got himself a little business there.''

The deputy wordlessly downed the hot coffee in two gulps and again nodded at Billy on his way out.

"Now, where was I? Oh, yeah. Start from the very beginning, Billy, and don't leave out a detail. This is for official records.''

Billy cleared his throat and went into the details of his trip to Bent Rock, telling about having shared his breakfast table with the Brogen gang in Las Cumbres. He then jumped to the incident at the train station in Bent Rock, when the Arabian bolted free and he had to give chase. No longer taking notes, the marshal followed Billy's story, barely breathing for fear of missing something of his adventure, and it was only after reaching the point where Billy threw his knife into Brogen that the lawman took a deep breath and relaxed.

''Whew! That's quite a story, Billy. You're aware, aren't you, that the Rocking J and the Dobie Girl both have put up some reward money for that bunch of rustlers you cleaned out back there? I sure hope our little bank has enough cash on hand to make good all you have coming.''

While Billy and the marshal were drinking coffee and discussing the rustlers, the door opened abruptly and Josh entered the small office with a look of grave concern on his face. Following close behind him was Paul Sanderson, who only gave Billy a cursory glance and avoided eye contact with him as he shut the door behind him.

After polite nods were exchanged among the four men in the room, Sanderson clenched his hat tightly in his hands and said, ''Billy . . . son, I never was very good at apologies, but I had a long talk with Becky last night, and it appears that I have done you a great injustice. I let my sister influence my judgement—without gathering all the facts and hearing your side of it. I'm begging you to forgive an old fool and come back to the Rocking J with us . . . please.''

Billy could feel the remorse in the ranch owner's apology, and concluded that he was indeed deeply affected by his action of firing him without first giving the facts the proper consideration. Yet, if he returned with him to the ranch he would find himself still on another's payroll when his very instincts told him he should now strike out on his own while he had the motivation and the funds.

"I suppose anybody could have made the same mistake, sir, and I appreciate your coming here to apologize personally, but I think it high time I cut my own trail. Hear there might be some good grazing land to be had farther north a-ways, and I guess I'll be checking it out. No hard feelings, I hope."

"Oh, I am disappointed you do not wish to return to the Rocking J, to be sure, and I can even appreciate the fact you wish to strike out on your own. I was the same way at your age. However, I am in a position to help you get started with your own place—that is, if you will accept my offer of help."

"I was never one to refuse a genuine offer of help, sir, and I'll keep that in mind if I should ever need it."

"There is just one more thing, Billy," Paul Sanderson said with a grin. "There is someone waiting outside. I believe she said something about you promising to show her around the Rocking J."

Taking his hat and heading for the door in a bound, Billy said, "Well, I guess that trip up north can be put off for a few days yet."